PARALLEL LIVES

By Lori Lucero

I0684349

To my family for all their love and support.

Prologue

She shouldn't have had a soda after dinner. Her mother had pointed that out in her overly-solicitous manner, but in true adolescent form, the girl chose to ignore her. She didn't think it was that big of a deal, but she'd tossed and turned before finally falling asleep almost an hour later than usual. And now, in the middle of the night, her nearly bursting bladder woke her. She stumbled to the bathroom. When she returned to her bedroom, she realized she somehow hadn't noticed how dark it was when she'd rushed for the bathroom, but now she could barely see her hand in front of her face. She'd almost made it to her bed when she bumped into her nightstand, spilling the glass of water on it. Besides getting her feet and the rug wet, water also splashed on the power strip on the floor, though in the dark, she didn't notice. Several outlets on the strip were unused, but her alarm clock, bedside light, and other small electronic items were plugged in on it.

"Dammit!" she sputtered. She groped for the bedside lamp. As she pressed the switch, she felt a shock go through her body.

Chapter One

Why do I answer the phone when I know it's Josh? Jen asked herself as she listened to her soon-to-be ex-husband's ranting. She really wished she hadn't asked him to help with Aquarius' vet bill, even as a loan.

"Look, Jen," Josh said now, his tone oozing false sympathy. "Obviously, worrying about the cat is a bit much for you right now. Why don't you let Libby and me take her? You know I love Aquarius, and Libby loves animals."

Horrorstruck, Jen felt her temper spiral out of control. "I had Aquarius before we got married, and I'd take her and go into hiding before I'd let you guys take her!"

Ignoring her tone, Josh said, "Animals can sense unhappiness. Why worry about the cat right now, when you're so upset? Libby will quit her job when we get married, so she'll be able to spend lots of time with her."

"Whose fault is it that I'm upset?" Jen countered. "If you and Libby want a cat, go down to the damned shelter and get a cat. There are loads down there. The only reason you're giving me a hard time about Aquarius now is so you'll get a better settlement. You never even paid attention to her. So go get another cat if Libby wants one and you want to score points for being a sensitive animal-loving guy. She already stole my husband; she won't get my goddamned cat too!"

After she hung up on him, Jen waited, half-expecting him to call back, but he didn't.

Jen awoke the next morning with the same feeling of dread that had plagued her every morning since Josh left her six months ago. She wanted to call in sick and go back to sleep, but the principal had already warned her about her absences. She forced herself to get up and stand under the shower, but skipped the dreaded ritual of stepping on the scale. She'd suffered enough angst lately, not to mention the fact that the angst led to stress eating. Just as she stepped out of the shower, Aquarius made a tell-tale retch. "Not now!" she groaned, as Aquarius hacked up a hairball. Aquarius always did this when she was running late. She suspected Josh forgot about hairballs and litter boxes when he was attempting to steal the cat from her.

She and Josh were never what anyone considered a match made in heaven. They met in Vegas when Jen was vacationing there with her friend Amy and were married on Jen's thirty-fifth birthday after knowing each other for only four months. Amy and her other friends had tried to discourage her from marrying him so soon, plus they didn't really like the guy.

"He's too smooth," they warned. "He'll break your heart."

Well, they were right on the money about that, Jen reflected bitterly, though at the time she wondered whether her less-sincere friends secretly thought Josh was out of her league. She knew Josh's friends thought that. But Jen was sure she knew what she was doing. Her feelings were helped along, she could see now, by the fact that she was turning thirty-five and wanted kids. She'd thought Josh might be her last chance.

What a crock, she thought. Here she was, thirty-seven, with no kids, having found out after they married that Josh didn't want kids after all. So now she'd lost even more time.

The day didn't improve much after she arrived at work, but nothing major happened until the principal called right after school let out.

"I need to see you in my office right away," Arabella said.

Jen wondered what was up. Ordinarily she liked Arabella, but she'd been on Jen's case lately. Jen admitted to herself that she'd been absent too much this school year, but Arabella had already spoken to her about that and she hadn't missed any work since. So now what?

The door to Arabella's office was open. With some trepidation, Jen walked in.

About twenty years older than Jen, Arabella had been the principal of Riverside Middle School for the last ten years, a few years longer than Jen had worked there. Her short, plump figure suggested a greater concern with work than working out. She'd been working in education for around thirty years and thus tended to be more old-school in her approach than some of her younger colleagues. She could be abrupt and somewhat formal, which Jen had found off-putting at first, but she truly cared about the students and teachers.

Right now, though, it was clear Arabella hadn't called Jen down to the office to express concern about her.

"Shut the door, please," said Arabella, not bothering with a greeting.

Jen did, though she wasn't happy about it. Arabella's tone was not friendly, and discussions with one's boss which require a closed door never bode well.

Arabella got right to the point. "Jen, I've tried to be patient. I know you're going through a tough time. You've been better about not missing work. I know things have been difficult. But when a parent comes and complains to me about profanity in your classroom—"

"WHAT?" Jen interrupted. There had to be some mistake. She never swore in the classroom, nor had any of the kids. At least not recently.

"Justin Bronson's mother came in and told me that Justin saw the word 'asshole' on your cell phone. . ."

Jen's face paled and her jaw dropped. Arabella couldn't help but notice.

"So is it true then?"

"No one was supposed to see that. . .it comes up when my ex calls. . ." Jen's face went white to scarlet.

"But a student did see it," Jen could see that Arabella was trying to stifle a smile, but at the same time, that she wouldn't just let this go. "And you shouldn't really have had your cell phone out during class time anyway."

"I didn't talk on it during class—" Jen protested.

But the meeting went downhill from there. When Jen finally escaped, it was all she could do not to burst into tears. She went into her classroom to grab her purse and planner and shut down her computer. Then she went into the teacher's lounge to check her mailbox, where she ran into Amy, literally.

"Hey, Jen, sorry! You okay?"

Jen gave in and burst into tears.

Amy put her arms around her and guided her to the couch. Other teachers passing through beat a hasty exit. Her co-workers had been great, but many had been on the receiving end of a few too many drama-queen episodes lately. And it took Jen a disproportionate amount of time to calm down. It wasn't like she'd been fired or gotten a bad evaluation. Still, it was embarrassing, and now Arabella was upset with her.

Once Jen calmed down enough to tell Amy what happened, she saw Amy, like Arabella, stifling a smile. "It's not funny," Jen moaned. "I'm in big trouble!"

"I know; I'm sorry, " Amy apologized. "It's just that I can't believe you programmed your cell to say that." Amy couldn't suppress a laugh. "Not that it's not fitting."

Despite herself, Jen smiled a little too. "It sure is. Yesterday he started in again about giving him Aquarius."

"Why the hell does he want Aquarius?"

"He doesn't. He's just using her as a bargaining chip. He's dragging her into this whole mess so that he can relent later and say 'hey, you got the cat like you wanted,' and use that as a reason to give me less money. And he's mad because I never got my master's—he always nagged me about how I should do that when we were married. He says I wouldn't need as much of his money if my job paid better. Like he doesn't have plenty of money. He's just cheap."

"'Asshole' is right," Amy said.

"I know," said Jen, and then, despite herself, she began to giggle. Amy joined in, and then soon they were both laughing hysterically.

Jen felt much better when she left the teacher's lounge with Amy a few minutes later. Talking with Amy could do that for her. Amy was her rock. It had been that way ever since they started teaching at Riverside, where they'd met as new teachers several years ago. In a school where most of the teachers were married with small children, it was great to have another single woman around the same age, especially since Jen was new in town and didn't know many people yet. Outgoing and fun, Amy helped the more introverted Jen come out of her shell. With her trim figure, long black hair, chocolate brown eyes, and porcelain skin, the gorgeous Amy never had trouble getting guys' attention, but unlike Jen, she expressed little desire to get married and start a family. "I *like* being able to come and go as I please," she always told Jen. "Kids are great, but they tie you down."

Though Amy had never liked Josh, she'd tried to get along with him for Jen's sake. At the time, Jen had wondered if maybe Amy saw Josh as taking Jen away from her. She thought Amy might be jealous. Now she realized that was ridiculous. Amy wasn't the jealous type. She was, however, a keen judge of character.

She and Amy walked out to the parking lot together and got into their respective cars. But Jen's car wouldn't start. *Damned piece of junk,* she thought. She'd owned the thing for almost ten years, but she couldn't afford a new one. She glanced out the window to see if Amy had driven off yet. Damn! She had. Jen rummaged through her purse for her cell phone. She found it and tried to turn it on, but the battery was dead. She rummaged through the glove compartment for her car charger, but couldn't find it for some reason.

The cheering up with Amy undone, she burst into tears. Again.

"I hate my life!" she screamed aloud, pounding the steering wheel. "I hate Josh, and teaching, and I hate that I have no family of my own, and that I never got my master's, and that I don't have more money. I hate my apartment and everything in it except Aquarius. I wish I could just start over!"

Jen got out of the car and slammed the door. She could hardly see, she was crying so hard. She and Amy spent so much time in the teacher's lounge that it had gotten rather late, and so when she tried the doors of the school they were locked. She groaned as she remembered she left her lanyard with her school ID and her key on it in her room. Not only that, but it started to rain, the rain mingling with her tears. She had no umbrella, and no choice but to walk a few blocks to a convenience store where there was a pay phone.

There was little traffic right around the school. The late buses carrying the kids from after-school activities had all left. She sensed increasing speeds and traffic as she got out of the school zone, but in her distraught state it hardly registered. She barely looked up as she crossed a busy street, until a blaring horn caught her attention.

The last thing she remembered seeing was Arabella behind the wheel, face frozen in horror.

***

First there was blackness, for what seemed an interminable amount of time. A sensation of floating through space. Was she dead? She figured she probably was. That bitch Libby was going to get Aquarius after all. She could hear an annoying buzzing sound, like an alarm clock. Were there alarm clocks in Heaven? Maybe she was in hell. Did people go to hell for programming their cell phones to read "asshole" whenever their ex called and then leaving it out for impressionable kids to see (never mind that it surely wasn't Justin's first experience with the word)?

The buzzing sound would not go away. Finally she opened her eyes. She could hardly believe what she saw. Her brain could not interpret the information.

I must be dead, she thought. Confusion and disorientation kept her brain spinning in circles, though she was no longer floating. She was in a twin bed rather than her own queen-size bed, in a room that looked like a teenager's bedroom. A laptop computer sat on the desk, which also contained a cell phone with a hot pink cover. Unframed posters tacked up on the walls instead of her own inexpensive prints. It looked like . . .

Jen sat up to get a better look, even though her disorientation made her dizzy and sitting up made it worse. *This is crazy.* That was the only thought in her brain for several minutes. She closed her eyes until the dizziness subsided. After a few minutes, she cautiously opened them again.

The room looked like a version of her childhood bedroom. It wasn't exactly like her old bedroom, but it was similar. It had the same color scheme she and her mother had picked out years ago— cream-colored furniture and walls with lavender accents, soft lavender rug, as well as the same general layout. But the posters, rather than being of 80s icons like Rick Springfield or Duran Duran, were of people she didn't recognize. Of course she didn't have a cell phone or laptop back in the day, and instead of her old stereo system with the turntable and tape deck, there was a CD player.

I must be dead. She could imagine no other way to explain what she saw. But who would have thought being dead could feel like having a hangover? She'd always assumed being dead meant not feeling any bodily sensations anymore. And she felt plenty now. The dizziness had subsided somewhat, but now her head was starting to pound.

The buzzing sound penetrated her consciousness again. It was coming from the alarm next to her bed. She turned it off just as her sister, Melanie, burst into the room from next door.

"I thought you were never going to turn that off," Melanie said.

Jen stared at her. This Melanie looked about eleven years old. The real Melanie was a thirty-five-year-old computer programmer who lived a few hours away from her. It had been several months since Jen had seen her. The real Melanie did not burst into her bedroom from the room next door in her pajamas.

Not since they were kids.

But then, that's exactly what Melanie looked like. With long, straight blond hair that wasn't the same style as she had worn when she was really eleven in the 80s, this Melanie was prepubescent, skinny, and her pajamas sagged on her.

"Melanie? Are you dead too?" Jen asked. What other explanation could there be?

"What are you talking about? Of course I'm not dead. What kind of bad dream did you have?"

"I don't know," said Jen. Maybe that's what *this* was, some kind of crazy dream. Ignoring her throbbing headache, she managed to get out of bed without falling despite her lingering dizziness. Slowly she walked over to the mirror. "Oh my God," she gasped in horror.

"You don't look that bad," said Melanie. "But you'll have to hurry if you want to take a shower."

"No, I know, it's just . . ." Jen groped for words.

What on earth was happening?

There, in the mirror, she no longer saw a thirty-seven-year-old woman staring back at her.

Herself, yes. But herself at age thirteen. Give or take.

Everything went black again.

***

"Mom, she just passed out!" Melanie shrieked. "What's wrong with her?"

"Melanie, calm down. Let me take a look at her. Jen?"

Jen opened her eyes and saw her mother's face. Well, sort of. Had her mother had a face lift or something? She looked so much younger—

Wait.

Melanie looked like a kid again. Jen looked like a kid again. Her mother looked like she had when Jen and Melanie were kids, more or less, although she looked to be in better shape and thus prettier, and with an updated hairstyle.

Had she gone back in time somehow?

But how could she have? She'd seen the laptop computer and the cell phone on her desk. These things were not around in the 80s, at least not in anything like their current form.

Were they all dead? Or maybe she was dreaming. That must be it. She vaguely remembered—was she hit by a car? She was probably in a coma—

"Jen? Say something," her mother demanded urgently.

"I-I'm okay," Jen managed to croak out.

"Thank goodness," her mother said. "You were starting to scare me. What happened?"

"I don't know," Jen replied shakily. "I just got up and went to the mirror and then everything went black."

"Maybe you have low blood sugar or something," her mom said. "Or you might be anemic. Melanie, go get Jen some juice. Jen, I'll help you get back into bed." As she did so, she noted, "Jen, you really should be more careful." She indicated a damp spot on the floor and picked up a water glass lying beside it. "You should move this." She waved her hand at the power strip close to the damp spot. "It could have gotten wet and you could have electrocuted yourself. Did you get a shock? Is that what happened?"

"No," Jen said. "I didn't even touch the power strip or try to turn on anything plugged into it."

"Okay, good." Her mother flipped the switch on the strip to the "off" position and unplugged it. "Let's give this one time to dry out in case some water did get in the outlets. I'll get you another one to use, but put it somewhere else, okay? Someplace where you won't spill anything on it."

"Okay, sure," Jen replied, too dazed to really pay attention to her mother's words. She did feel better once her mother helped her back into bed. Her brain was still spinning, but at least she didn't feel like she would black out again. Melanie brought her some apple juice, which she sipped. The cat jumped onto the bed with her. *Wait a minute.*

She hadn't owned a cat growing up.

This cat looked just like Aquarius.

Well, if she was in a coma, she supposed she could dream about anything. Why not dream she was a kid again, but a kid when there were laptop computers, cell phones, and Aquarius?

"Aquarius?" she asked aloud. "What are you doing here?"

"She always likes to be by you," said Melanie, who still stood beside her bed. "You must *really* be sick."

"Maybe I should stay home with you," her mother said.

"No, really, I feel a lot better already," said Jen. She'd probably be waking up from this dream/coma soon anyway. "I just need to rest."

"Well, I don't know." Her mother hesitated.

"Maybe you could come home at lunch," Jen suggested. Her mom used to do that sometimes when they were sick.

"I suppose I could do that. Still, I think I should take you to the doctor when I get home from work. And I want you to call me if you need anything."

"Okay," agreed Jen. She didn't exactly feel up to arguing. Her head was still spinning.

Her mom and Melanie left the room to finish getting ready for work and school. Her mother poked her head in once more before leaving for work, to make sure Jen was really all right with being alone for a few hours. Jen reassured her mother she felt much better and just needed to rest awhile.

"Well, okay," said her mother, obviously reluctant to leave. "I'll see you at lunch then."

As soon as everyone cleared out of the house, Jen got out of bed. Her dizziness had mostly subsided and her headache had dulled. Still, she felt weird. Lighter. Smaller. More energetic, like she didn't want to sit still, but oddly discombobulated. Glancing down at her hands, she noticed remnants of purple nail polish on her fingernails. She hadn't worn fingernail polish since college.

She felt strangely lucid in this dream. But it probably wasn't really just a dream. She was probably either in a coma or dead. So she supposed it made sense that she felt different than she would if she were merely dreaming.

She carefully avoided the mirror over her dresser since it was so bizarre to see the younger version of herself staring back.

If she stepped outside her bedroom, would she see the proverbial white light?

The thought terrified her. It made her afraid to open the door, but finally, slowly, she turned the knob. She eased the door open a half inch.

No white light.

Just an ordinary hallway.

Jen breathed a deep sigh of relief. Sure, her life sucked lately. But she didn't want to be dead. No white light meant there was at least a chance she was just in a coma and might come out of it.

Cautiously, she stepped into the hallway. Interestingly, from here, her Coma-World house looked much the same as her real childhood home. The cream-colored carpet, the pictures on the walls. But upon closer inspection, she saw that the pictures were different. Instead of the picture of herself at age six, her sister at four, and her brother at age two, for example, there was a picture of just her and her sister at those ages. Where was her brother? Had the Coma-World obliterated him?

She ran through the rooms upstairs. Melanie's bedroom. The bathroom they shared. Her parents' room, with the adjoining bath. Finally, though, she went into the room that caused her to breathe a sigh of relief.

This room was obviously the room of a small boy, maybe four years old, judging from the pictures on the wall and the toys. So probably he just hadn't been born yet when the picture in the hall was taken. Jen sighed in relief. Her brother hadn't been obliterated in her Coma-World, if that's what this was. He was just born later, further apart in age from her and Melanie.

What does it matter? None of this is real anyway. But Jen still felt better somehow, seeing her brother's room.

She went downstairs, figuring she could more closely examine the upstairs rooms later. Again, the living room and kitchen were laid out much like they had been in her childhood home, but there were some small differences. The appliances and furniture were updated, more like the ones her mom owned now than the ones they'd had when Jen was growing up. The morning paper was still sitting on the kitchen table. March 5, 2012, the date read.

The last day she could remember in her real life was Wednesday, February 29th. Was her subconscious trying to tell her how much time had passed? Had she just not dreamed anything in the intervening days? She remembered the sensation of floating in blackness for a long time. She hadn't even known people dreamed while in a coma. She'd heard of people in comas being able to hear people talking to them and things like that, but she'd never heard of anything like this. This dream, assuming it was a dream and she wasn't dead, was terrifyingly specific.

But maybe the newspaper date didn't mean anything.

She went to the hutch, where she figured her mother still kept their baby books.

She smiled when she realized that her mother hadn't altered this practice in the Coma-World. She pulled out the three baby books, one for her, one for Melanie, and one for their brother Ben. She looked at her own first. The birth certificate interested her the most. It had her name, Jennifer Lynelle Edwards, and date of birth—August 26, 1998—

She stared at it in disbelief. The August 26th part was the same as it had always been. But she had been born in 1974, not 1998.

The Coma-World was getting weirder and weirder.

She looked at the birth certificate again. She hadn't read it wrong. This said she was born in 1998.

She looked at the rest of it. The place of birth was also different. She had been born in Great Falls, Montana, in 1974, but this said she was born in Riverside, Washington, where in actuality she had been living for the last several years.

When staring at the birth certificate for several minutes didn't change anything, she closed her own baby book and opened Melanie's. Her birth date was also different. Instead of being born in 1976, this said she was born in 2000. According to this Coma-World birth certificate, she, too, had been born in Riverside, WA. Ben's birth certificate said that he had been born in 2007 rather than 1978, also in Riverside.

Her head was starting to spin again. Her stomach felt queasy. Thinking she was about to be sick, she raced for the bathroom, but when she got there, the feeling had mostly passed. She sat down on the floor and put her head between her knees for a few minutes until she felt better. Sitting there, she noticed a scale by the toilet. She just had to check.

She smiled at the number. *Well*, she thought, *I guess the Coma-World isn't all bad!*

Jen went back into her bedroom. *I'll get into bed and go back to sleep,* she thought. *I'll wake up in a hospital bed and my friends and family will be there.*

***

"Well, hello, Aquarius." Her mother's voice woke Jen. She opened her eyes. She was not in a hospital bed. No, this was Coma-World continued. Jen groaned.

Coma-Mom was still talking softly to Aquarius. "How's your mommy?"

It was strange to hear Coma-Mom talking to Aquarius like a member of the family. Her real mother had met Aquarius exactly once. Usually Jen went to visit her real mother rather than vice versa, and she never brought Aquarius, since cats didn't travel well.

Coma-Mom knocked softly on her door. "Jen?"

"Hi, Mom," Jen called out.

"How are you doing, honey?" Coma-Mom asked as she entered the room with a Subway bag on her arm and a soda in her hand.

"Better," said Jen, though her stomach still felt queasy. She smiled slightly though, as she realized that Coma-Mom knew that Subway was her favorite.

"Have you eaten anything today?"

"No," Jen admitted.

"You'd better eat this then," said Coma-Mom. "Do you feel like getting up, or do you just want to eat this here?"

"I'll come downstairs," Jen said.

As Jen entered the kitchen, Coma-Mom was already sitting at the table, eating her own lunch. Jen's eye was immediately drawn to Coma-Mom's outfit.

"Why are you wearing nurse's scrubs?" she asked.

"Uh, I'm a nurse, what did you think?"

"I thought you were a retired secretary who lived in Montana," Jen blurted out.

"What are you talking about?"

"You know—Montana? Where I was born and grew up? Where you still live?" Jen glanced down at the newspaper, still on the table. There was something else important about it besides the date that hadn't registered when she had first looked at it. It wasn't the *Great Falls Tribune,* her hometown newspaper, but rather the *Riverside Herald.*

"Uh, noooo." Coma-Mom was now looking at her in a very concerned way. "You were born right here in Riverside. You've never even been to Montana, though I did grow up there."

Jen shook her head disbelievingly. "No, I was born in Montana. I didn't move here until I was twenty-nine years old. None of this is real."

Coma-Mom's look changed from concern to alarm. "Jen, you're thirteen years old. You're not making any sense. And you know you were born in Riverside."

Jen shook her head again. This was getting ridiculous. "No, I moved to Riverside when I was twenty-nine. I'm thirty-seven now. I was hit by a car a few days ago. I think I've been in a coma ever since. That's why this dream is insanely long and probably why I felt like I was just floating in blackness for a really long time. But none of this could possibly be real."

Now Coma-Mom looked panicked. "I'm going to call the doctor's office and tell them I'm not coming in for the rest of the afternoon," she said, reaching for her phone. "And then we're going straight to the emergency room. I think you may have sustained a head injury when you passed out this morning!"

Chapter Two

Several hours later Jen was severely pissed off. There had been no reasoning with Coma-Mom once she decided Jen might have a head injury. Before Jen realized what was happening, she was in the passenger seat of Coma-Mom's car, being driven to the emergency room at top speed. Jen was surprised Coma-Mom didn't get a speeding ticket.

Then they'd had to wait. It wasn't like Jen was bleeding from the head, so she wasn't considered high priority. While they sat on uncomfortable ER waiting room chairs, Jen tried to make herself wake up. But while she could do that for regular dreams sometimes, she was unable to do so now. Apparently it wasn't as easy to make yourself come out of a coma. Coma-Mom tried to talk to her, but Jen just kept saying, "I need to wake up; this isn't real!" Which didn't reassure Coma-Mom.

The little Jen had seen of her that day suggested someone competent and in control—less mousy than her real mom—but nothing in Coma-Mom's training or experience had prepared her for her daughter's apparent mental breakdown. She pleaded with Jen to talk to her and kept trying to jog her memory—"Jen, remember the time we all—" until Jen felt like the worst daughter ever for putting her through this, even if it couldn't be real.

Of course, none of the family memories her mother brought up were at all familiar to Jen. Eventually she said, "Mom, can I just rest for a while?" If Coma-Mom didn't stop talking, they'd both go insane. This seemed to break through Coma-Mom's anxiety and she agreed resting would probably be a good idea. Though not tension-free, Jen relaxed in the blissful silence.

When they finally got in to see the doctor, he asked Jen and her mom about symptoms commonly associated with head injuries. No, she wasn't nauseated, dizzy (anymore), or drowsy. Her headache was gone, and she didn't even mention it since she knew the fall wasn't what caused it. The doctor found a slight bump on her head from when she'd passed out that morning, but it didn't even hurt. Blood tests ruled out anemia, which could have caused her to feel lightheaded enough to faint in the first place.

"But she's extremely confused!" Coma-Mom exclaimed. "She was talking pure nonsense before I brought her here. She told me she's thirty-seven years old and she's in a coma now. She can't remember things she's known all her life about her background. She tried to tell me she grew up in Montana when she's never even been there. She didn't even remember I'm a nurse."

"Jennifer, have you been using drugs, young lady?" Coma-Doc asked.

"No, of course not!" Jen snapped.

"Jennifer, don't be rude. I don't think she's been using any drugs, doctor," Coma-Mom said. "I haven't noticed any changes in behavior until today. None at all. And Jen is normally very well-behaved."

Despite their denials, Coma-Doctor suggested to Coma-Mom that it might be a good idea to test for common street drugs, just in case, and, much to Jen's indignation, Coma-Mom agreed. When the drug testing came back negative, Coma-Doctor ordered a CT scan, as well as a psych consult. It was about then that fear started to break through Jen's anger.

Why couldn't she wake up? Was this really some bizarre dream, or was she actually dead?

This did not sound like anything she'd ever read about or seen on TV regarding near-death experiences. Jen supposed anything was possible, but if she were dead, why wasn't she seeing dead relatives? She'd only seen her mother and sister, who were still alive, albeit twenty-plus years older than they were appearing to her now.

If it was a dream, it was incredibly long. Though if she were in a coma, she supposed she could be having an incredibly long dream.

What else could be going on?

The CT scan wasn't unpleasant, though Jen wasn't in the mood to completely still, even for a few minutes. At least that calmed her down a bit, though she still wasn't happy. She tried to think. After the test, she had to talk to the psychiatrist. What if he decided to hospitalize her? She shuddered inwardly at the thought of spending time on an adolescent psych ward. Maybe—for now at least—she should just play along. Play along and act as if this—situation—were real, at least until she could figure out what to do next.

***

Later that night, Jen sat in her room, relieved to be alone. Her mother hadn't let her out of her sight the whole evening, convinced Jen would say or do something bizarre again at any moment. Since Jen decided to play along, the psychiatrist thought she seemed to be in touch with reality, not depressed, maybe a little anxious, but not a danger to herself or others. He was concerned about the possibility Jen might have experienced some sort of brief psychotic episode, based on what her mother said, and wanted her mother to schedule a follow-up appointment for Jen with him through his private practice. In any case, he said, she should call again immediately if she observed any disturbing behavior. The CT scan results would be sent to Jen's pediatrician. Jen's mother was to schedule a follow-up appointment to review the results as soon as possible.

Now everyone had gone to bed, but Jen didn't feel sleepy, so she decided to explore her room for clues regarding her current existence. At the foot of her bed was a purple backpack. She opened it up and pulled out a planner. She recognized the planner, not because she had owned one, but because it was the planner used at Riverside, the middle school where Jen taught.

Oh. My. God. Was she really a student at Riverside?

She supposed she should have thought of this, but she hadn't. She had been sure she would wake up any minute, for one thing.

She opened the planner. On the inside, her name and a computer printout of her schedule were taped to the inside cover. The schedule had her name, an ID number, and her grade level. Supposedly she was an 8th-grader at Riverside Middle School. Riverside had block scheduling, and her first block of the day was Language Arts and History with Ms. Whiteside.

This was definitely worth another Oh. My. God.

Her first two hours of the day would be spent with her best friend, whom she knew as Amy, but would now have to call Ms. Whiteside. She'd have to be careful not to call her Amy by accident.

"I can't do this!" Jen exclaimed aloud. She had done her time as a middle school student. How could she do it all over again? Having to call her friends and colleagues by their last names. Trying to fit in among a bunch of thirteen and fourteen-year-olds whose behavior she knew for a fact was ridiculous.

And what if she couldn't pass the new state assessment exam and couldn't graduate high school? *THAT would be the ultimate irony.*

Sure, she taught some reading and writing prompts for the standardized test, though at the middle school level rather than at the high school level, but she hadn't studied any math or science for a long time—

But if she was somehow stuck here, she guessed that would change.

Visions of an inpatient unit swam in her head. She had to play along. At least for now.

***

The loud buzz pierced her consciousness, along with a Rick Springfield song. Again, Melanie burst through the door connecting their rooms.

"Why do you like that 80s retro crap so much?" she demanded.

"Can you let me wake up before you start bugging me?" Jen mumbled.

"So are you going to go to school today or what?" Melanie asked. "Mom said you had to go to the emergency room yesterday, but then you didn't seem sick last night."

"I feel a lot better," Jen said. "Mom was just worried because I fainted yesterday morning. And I guess I'd better go to school today."

This was a horrible thought, but she didn't know what else to do. Feigning illness would just cause her parents greater concern.

After showering, she searched her closet for something to wear. She didn't feel comfortable with most of the clothing options she saw, given they were for a thirteen-year-old girl rather than a thirty-seven-year-old woman. Also, they looked so tiny. How could she ever fit into any of these things?

Then she remembered the number on the scale yesterday and smiled. The clothes should fit at least. She finally found something that wasn't too offensive but would still blend in among the other students. In trying to do something with her hair and makeup, she thought she looked somewhat better than she had when she was thirteen the first time. But maybe she was just happy to see a thinner version of herself, after all the stress eating.

She sure didn't feel like stress eating now, though. If anything, the thought of what she would soon face made her want to throw up.

"Jen, hurry," Melanie called. "We're going to miss the bus!"

So they took the bus to school. Jen hadn't even been sure of that. She knew where the school was, of course, but she hadn't known if they lived far enough away so they would take the bus or not.

"Coming," she called. With one last glance at herself in the mirror, she grabbed her backpack and hurried downstairs.

"Jen, aren't you going to eat something?" her mother asked. "You don't want to get lightheaded again."

Jen went to the kitchen cupboard and grabbed a granola bar to eat on the way.

"Okay, " her mother said. "Are you sure you're feeling okay?"

"Yep—never better," Jen insisted, managing to project a confidence she didn't feel.

"All right—have a good day."

"Come on, Jen!" Melanie said.

"All right, all right." She followed Melanie out the door.

"You're always so slow," Melanie complained.

"Well, you don't have to wait for me," Jen pointed out.

"Maybe tomorrow I won't," Melanie retorted.

Jen was glad Melanie had waited today, at least. She didn't even know where the bus stop was.

"Why are you such a ray of sunshine this morning?" she asked Melanie.

"Oh—I think Keaton likes someone else. He didn't answer my text last night, and then I tried to call him and kept getting his voice mail. So then I called Kim, and she said she saw him with

Ashley and she thinks Keaton likes her. Even though he swore to me he didn't!" Melanie said indignantly.

"But Melanie, you're—" Jen started, then stopped. In their adult lives Melanie had sometimes called Jen to complain about or ask for advice regarding her love life, but never about men.

Melanie was a lesbian.

But, she remembered now, Melanie had some crushes on and even dated some boys and young men before she figured this out.

And if Melanie hadn't figured it out yet, Jen wouldn't enlighten her. She groped for something to say.

"Well, have you been able to talk to Keaton? Maybe he was just busy last night."

"Well, maybe," said Melanie, but she didn't seem convinced.

The bus pulled up, saving Jen from any further conversation. They had almost reached the bus stop and hurried to get there in time.

When they got on the bus, Melanie found someone to sit with right away, but Jen looked around uncertainly. And then she saw someone she recognized.

Lucy Morrison was a student of hers last year, in seventh grade. Lucy had major emotional problems at the time and Jen and a school counselor helped her through it. Lucy was sitting alone, so Jen went up to her seat and asked if she could sit there.

"I guess—if you want to," Lucy replied.

Lucy didn't sound too enthusiastic, but Jen tried not to take it personally. Lucy tended to sound that way in general, she remembered. She sat down next to Lucy, but then felt awkward. She wasn't sure if she should introduce herself or what.

Maybe they'd already met. Well, they had, in Jen's "real" life, but she had no idea whether they'd met in this one.

"You're that new girl, who moved here a few months ago. I think you're in my art class. Jen, is it?" Lucy saved her from possibly making a fool of herself.

"Yes, Jen. And you're Lucy."

"Yep, that's me."

Awkward silence. Jen tried to think of a way to start a conversation without acting like she knew Lucy. But before she could, Lucy asked her a question.

"Where did you move here from?"

"Seattle," Jen answered. She wouldn't have even known that if Melanie hadn't mentioned it last night at dinner. She'd seen no unpacked boxes around the house indicating a recent move. She hoped Lucy didn't ask her too many questions about living there. She had only visited Seattle a few times since moving to Washington State.

"It sucks that you had to move here—it must have been great to live there," said Lucy.

"I guess," said Jen. "There were a lot of cool things to do, but I hated the gray and rainy weather. At least it's sunnier here, most of the time anyway."

Lucy shrugged. "Whatever." She turned back toward the window.

They fell silent for a moment, long enough for Jen to think Lucy wouldn't talk to her again, when Lucy said, "I just want to get away from here. Maybe I'll live in Seattle. Or maybe LA or someplace."

Jen could remember wanting to leave her hometown at Lucy's age, too. Of course, part of Lucy's longing to escape was due to a desire to be away from her dysfunctional family. Jen hadn't wanted to be away from her family, just her boring hometown.

"Lots of kids want to get away at your age," she said, then felt herself blush. She sounded totally patronizing.

And not at all like another thirteen-year-old.

"Excuse me, but aren't you the same age?" Lucy shot back.

"Sorry—I meant, our age," Jen stammered. "I mean, who doesn't want to go somewhere more exciting?"

Lucy seemed somewhat mollified by this response, but they didn't speak much during the rest of the bus ride. Jen was relieved when they arrived at school. Lucy didn't bother waiting for her once they got off the bus.

As she entered the school, panic seized her. Would it be laid out in the same way as in her real life? It looked the same on the outside, a relatively new (having opened in 2002) gray brick two-story building, with portable classrooms on one side. She breathed a small sigh of relief as she realized the inside of the school appeared to be the same as well. The library was directly across from the front doors; the main office off to the left.

She headed over toward where the 8th-grade wing should be, getting her planner out of her backpack as she went. This, too, appeared to be where she expected. She could see several eighth-grade teachers—her coworkers—in the hallway.

Suddenly she had to lean against the wall by the library for a moment as a feeling of disorientation made her dizzy again. *The school was exactly the same.* Why were the school and the people in it the same, while her life and that of her family—though her family seemed oblivious-had changed drastically?

She should have expected it. After all, she had a schedule with some of her coworkers as teachers. But seeing the school looking exactly the same and everyone in it carrying on like always, while her life was completely upended, was so surreal she couldn't absorb it right away.

"Honey, are you all right?" the school librarian's voice broke into her thoughts.

Jen looked up. Lisa Price, the librarian, had just opened the doors to the library and noticed Jen leaning against the wall. The librarian was the same, too. Of course she was.

"Do you need to go to the nurse's office?" Lisa asked, when Jen didn't respond.

That snapped Jen out of her stupor. If she went to see Amber, the school nurse (a lovely young woman in her early thirties, new to the school this year), Amber would call her mother, and her mother would panic, expecting Daughter's Mental Breakdown, Part II.

"I'm fine," she told Lisa. "I think I'm just getting my period or something, but I'm okay now."

"Okay, if you're sure."

"I am. Thanks." Jen hurried off.

When she was in school, she had always written her locker combination on the last page of her binder. She hadn't owned a school-issued planner then. Now as she perused her planner, she saw her locker number listed on her schedule, and when she turned to the last page, there was her combination. She sighed in relief. At least she wouldn't have to worry about getting into her locker. She knew the backpack wouldn't be allowed in class.

As she glanced down the hallway, she could see Amy outside her classroom, the same room she used in Jen's real life. She wondered who used her own classroom. Maybe she could run upstairs and find out at some point during her day.

As she deposited her backpack and jacket inside her locker, Jen realized she had another problem. She wouldn't know where to sit in any of her classes. She decided to wait until the last possible second to go into Amy's classroom. She had subbed for Amy a couple of times during her prep period, and she knew Amy had her students sit alphabetically. If she arrived when most students were already seated, she should be able to find the right seat.

When she did enter the classroom, it was easier than she thought, since she recognized some of the kids, having taught them last year. Just before the tardy bell rang, she slipped into the empty seat behind Patrick Davis.

Since the material wasn't exactly new to Jen, she didn't force herself to focus on it too closely. It was surreal being in Amy's class as a student. But Amy was a good teacher, and since the students were honors students, they behaved pretty well. The experience wasn't overly unpleasant.

About half an hour after class had started, an office aide brought in a new student. Amy spoke briefly with the aide and then introduced the student as Miguel Santos. He was from California. He was a good-looking kid, with dark, Latin looks as his name suggested. He caught Jen's eye and winked at her. Alarmed, Jen dropped her eyes to her desk top. That was all she needed, a thirteen-year-old with a crush on her.

Jen sat toward the back of the classroom, in the row closest to the door. The seat across from hers was the only empty seat, so Amy gave that seat to Miguel even though it messed up her alphabetical-order seating scheme.

For the rest of the class period, Miguel kept smiling and trying to catch her eye, and she kept trying to ignore him. The remaining hour and a half dragged. A note landed on her desk. She slipped it between the pages of her book. Finally the bell rang.

"What's your name?" Miguel asked her once they'd been dismissed.

"Jen," she said.

"It's great to meet you, Jen," he said. "Read my note, okay?" And with that, he sauntered off with thirteen-year-old cockiness.

Patrick Davis laughed at her. "Looks like someone thinks you're hot," he said.

"Shit!" she said, too loudly judging by the startled glances shot her way.

"Jennifer!" Amy said sharply.

"Sorry, M-Ms. Whiteside," Jen stammered. Shit, she'd almost called her Amy.

"I've talked to you before about your language," Amy said. "This time it's going to cost you 30 minutes of detention."

Fuck, Jen thought. She managed not to say it. If she ever got back to her real life, Amy would be in so much trouble. Of course, it would be pretty hard to explain to her *why* she was in so much trouble.

Double fuck.

***

Lunch was difficult. She sat alone in a corner, hoping no one would bother her. At least when she'd gone through middle school the first time she'd had friends. No one seemed to expect her to sit with them here.

"Is this seat taken?" She looked up to see Miguel standing there, lunch tray in hand.

She shouldn't encourage him. She knew she shouldn't. But looking at him standing there with such hope in his eyes, she couldn't hurt his feelings. "You can sit there," she said, smiling at him in a way she hoped was friendly but that he wouldn't interpret as flirtatious.

Miguel flashed her a dazzling smile and sat down. "Thanks," he said. "Are you new here too? Is that why you're sitting by yourself?"

"We moved here three months ago from Seattle," she said. "I guess it's taken me awhile to meet people."

"Yeah, it can take awhile to break into the cliques," Miguel agreed.

So the rest of her lunch period actually wasn't bad. Miguel wasn't like most thirteen-year-old boys. He was much more mature, intelligent and well-traveled. He had even gone to school abroad for a year.

She ran into Lucy Morrison again in art class, the one place she couldn't figure out where to sit. The class was seated four to a table for the most part, but the seating didn't appear to be alphabetical and quite a few empty seats remained when everyone was seated.

But then, the teacher unexpectedly saved her. "Jennifer, why don't you sit here with Lucy, since there's no one else at her table and everyone needs a partner today."

She sat down next to Lucy, who seemed to appreciate her company somewhat more than she had this morning. Jen had always been pretty good in art; maybe Lucy had seen some of the thirteen-year-old Jen's work and that's why she didn't mind being paired with her. If Jen remembered correctly, Lucy was quite artistic as well.

They worked together companionably on a mosaic for most of the period. Jen already knew that Lucy's parents divorced last year. She had to act like she didn't know, of course, but she talked a little bit about her family, remembering from her talks with Lucy last year the best ways to get her to open up, and Lucy mentioned the divorce, as well as family information that was new to Jen. Lucy's father had moved to California, and her mother had a new boyfriend who hung out at their house all the time.

"What's he like?" Jen asked, attempting to sound another kid rather than a teacher or counselor trying to get Lucy to process her feelings. That approach hadn't worked so well in the past with Lucy anyway.

Lucy shrugged. "He's okay, I guess." She didn't seem inclined to say much more about him, except that he and her mother often stayed out very late, even on weeknights. "Which is fine by me. I get the place to myself and can have my friends over or go out whenever I want. Mom never checks up on me like she used to."

Jen's heart sank. It sounded as though Lucy's situation had worsened. Things had been going a little better by the end of last school year, but the addition of this new boyfriend had apparently caused circumstances to take a nosedive. But what should she say? If she expressed dismay, Lucy would just shut her out. She decided to try another approach.

"So do you think your mom really likes this guy?"

Lucy thought about that for a moment. "Well, she's always with him, so I guess so. But mostly, she hates being alone."

The words hit a little close to home for Jen. Had she really been in love with Josh or was she just tired of being alone when all her friends were getting married and having babies? Some had been married for years or were on marriage number two.

Jen tried to think of a way to impart her life experience that sounded like how a thirteen-year-old might say it.

"I think it's kind of pathetic when someone goes out with a guy just to have a boyfriend," she said.

"Fucking pathetic," Lucy agreed, fortunately not loud enough for the teacher to hear.

Yes! They were bonding! Jen hoped she didn't screw up their fragile connection.

"So are your parents still together?" Lucy asked.

"Yeah." Jen wasn't sure if Lucy would get any references to Beaver Cleaver or the Brady Bunch, so she just said, "I guess we're lucky."

"Yeah, you are," Lucy said. "So I guess you didn't move here because of a divorce."

"Nope." Jen didn't know why they had moved here, actually. But she didn't have to explain, because Lucy didn't ask. Instead she asked about Jen's siblings, and Jen told her about Melanie and Ben.

"You are so lucky," Lucy said. "I wish I wasn't an only child. Actually, I wish I had an older brother who would introduce me to his friends."

Jen remembered from her conversations with Lucy last year that Lucy had said she was an "accident"; her mother hadn't even wanted her and her parents had only gotten married because Lucy's mother was pregnant with her. She had also spoken some with Lucy's mother, who independently brought up the fact that she married Lucy's father because she'd been pregnant at the time. It wasn't as though Jen would have asked her about it. She wasn't sure it was true Lucy's mother didn't want her, but she didn't seem to have adequate parenting skills. And now this new boyfriend was making things even worse.

"Well, maybe you can come over and hang out sometime," she said to Lucy. For sure Jen wouldn't go over there—even if Lucy did invite her—if Lucy was having a wild party or something, but maybe she could get Lucy to come over to her place so she could experience the positive influence of Jen's family.

"Yeah, maybe," Lucy sounded noncommittal.

"It's time to start cleaning up," Celeste—Jen had a hard time thinking of her colleagues as Ms. or Mr.—told the class.

"So who was that hot guy you were eating lunch with today?" Lucy asked as they started to clean up. They'd mostly finished their mosaic, and they would be able to complete it tomorrow easily.

"He's a new guy. His name is Miguel. I have a couple of classes with him," Jen said. She felt embarrassed at the thought of a thirteen-year-old crushing on her, even though she was, by outward appearances, also thirteen.

"Looks like he really likes you. You're lucky. I wish someone that hot was into me," said Lucy.

Jen also wished Miguel liked Lucy rather than her, but she thought Lucy would think her odd if she said so. She was saved from having to answer Lucy when the bell rang.

After art was the class Jen had been dreading all day. P.E.

Actually, since P.E. alternated with band, she didn't know what class she was supposed to go to that day. She stopped by the band room and told the band director she had been sick the day before and couldn't remember which one she had that day. It was just as well it wasn't band, since she had forgotten her flute. She *did* have her P.E. clothes in her locker, wrinkled and slightly smelly though they were.

There was nothing like changing clothes in the locker room before P.E. with a bunch of middle-schoolers to bring back the middle-school experience in terrifying detail. Even though she hadn't met them, she could pick out the popular girls by their looks and conversation. She shrank away from them, hoping to escape their notice and thus their ridicule.

Why do you care what they think? She asked herself. She was thirty-seven years old, for God's sake.

"Nice outfit, Jen! That is your name, isn't it?" A girl with long, blond hair taunted, to her friends' amusement. Jen thought one of the other girls had called the blond girl Brianna, and she seemed to be the ringleader of the popular girls.

Jen glanced down at her gym clothes. They were kind of gross, since it was clear they hadn't been washed since last worn, but they didn't look much different than anyone else's. And judging by the unwashed-adolescent odor permeating the air, she was sure she wasn't the only one whose clothes hadn't been washed.

Jen knew ignoring the girl would only cause her to increase her taunting. Quickly, she tried to think of something to say that wouldn't make things worse. "Thanks, what is it, Brianna?" she asked, smiling coolly at the blond girl and looking her straight in the eye.

Her approach seemed to work. Brianna turned away without saying anything to her. One of the other girls smiled and nodded at Jen once Brianna's back was turned.

Having the wisdom of a thirty-seven-year-old helps when you're navigating the middle-school world, Jen thought. When she was really thirteen, she would have tried to ignore someone like Brianna but been visibly upset, thus making things worse. She was sure Brianna would have loved to see her get upset.

Her pride was short-lived, however. Ms. Paine, the gym teacher, was aptly named. Even as a colleague, Jen thought of her as Ms. Paine rather than by her first name, June. A no-nonsense woman in her mid-fifties, Ms. Paine was known for making the kids run extra laps or do push-ups for the slightest infraction. All the kids hated her and called her Paine-in-the-Ass (not too original, but effective). She didn't seem to have friends among the faculty either.

Now Ms. Paine poked her head into the locker room and called, "Girls, get out here, you're late," in her shrill voice.

Great. The girls all trooped dutifully out into the gym. After taking attendance, Ms. Paine made all the girls run ten laps for being late. The boys were all on time, so they were spared the punishment. When the girls groaned, Ms. Paine said, "Do you want to try for twenty?" They all fell silent at that and started to run.

Jen couldn't remember the last time she had run anywhere. Her body felt light, in surprisingly good shape. It made running kind of fun, even though she had never enjoyed it before.

She groaned inwardly, though, when she realized what the activity would be for the day. Volleyball. She had always been horrible at volleyball. She couldn't serve at all. Forearm passes actually hurt her arms. She was decent at setting, but little else. She hadn't played in years and didn't miss it at all.

At least teams weren't picked the way they used to be. When Jen was in school, the gym teacher picked a couple of team captains, who then chose the kids they wanted on their team. t was a cruel system which made the less athletic and less popular kids feel like crap. These days even Ms. Paine was diplomatic enough to have the students count off.

This, however, did not make the experience of playing the game any better.

Jen was just standing there, zoning out, when Ms. Paine yelled, "Jen, get your head in the game!" which distracted her even more and caused her to get hit in the head with the ball, much to the other students' amusement. Another time, the ball was headed right toward her. "I've got it," she called, then promptly tripped over her own feet. Everyone laughed again when she fell. Middle-school students were such little shits, she thought. No compassion. She got to her feet, trying to ignore the pain in her right knee.

"Edwards, are you bleeding?" Ms. Paine bellowed.

It took a minute for Jen to realize Ms. Paine was talking to her, since she was used to going by her married name, Jensen. Finally she glanced down and saw she was in fact bleeding and there was some blood on the floor.

Screech! Ms. Paine's whistle blasted. "Everybody stay back." Her voice was that of someone who knew she must remain calm in the face of a dire emergency. "There's blood on the floor. What did we learn in our health lesson, students?"

"If it's warm, wet, and not yours, don't touch it," the students recited dutifully.

Jen could feel her face flaming. Was this necessary? Sure, they shouldn't touch her blood, but no one was even near her.

"Mendoza, go get the first aid kit in my office," Ms. Paine barked. Isabel Mendoza—a student of Jen's last year—scurried off to the locker room. Jen wasn't sure what to do other than stay frozen in place. She could feel the kids staring at her, whispering among themselves.

It seemed like forever, but it probably wasn't more than a minute or two before Isabel came back with the first aid kit. Ms. Paine donned a non-latex (to avoid allergic reactions, remember, students?) glove and took care of Jen's knee. She then sent Isabel to get the janitor to clean up the blood on the floor. By the time the floor was clean, there were only five minutes left before everyone had to change for their next class.

At least that was one good thing.

Now, finally, she had her last class of the day, her enrichment class with Amy. She didn't look forward to seeing her again after Amy had given her detention earlier in the day, but skipping the class would only make things worse.

Miguel was in this class too, and kept sneaking glances at her, but he wasn't sitting close to her, so it was easier to ignore him than it had been that morning.

Amy approached her desk at the end of class. "Jen, do you want to serve your detention today or tomorrow?"

"Can I just tell my sister I'll have to take the late bus and then get some homework from my locker?" Jen asked. Amy nodded, and Jen headed for the sixth-grade hallway. It took her awhile since the hallways were jammed with kids. As a teacher, she always avoided the hallways right after classes let out as much as possible. She managed to find Melanie and let her know she wouldn't be home until later, then grabbed some books from her locker.

Sitting there at her desk in Amy's classroom, she stole a glance at her friend. Did Amy have another best friend in this life? What was she like? Jen felt oddly envious of this theoretical best friend.

Amy caught her staring. "Jen, shouldn't you be getting some work done?"

"Sorry," Jen said, opening her literature book. As she did, she came across Miguel's note, which she had slid between the pages just before the story they were assigned to read. Quickly she stuffed it into her pocket. She didn't want Amy to catch her with it. She started reading the story, stealing glances at Amy as she did. It seemed to her that Amy looked stressed out, but maybe she was imagining things.

After today, maybe an adolescent psych ward doesn't sound so bad, Jen thought, after she'd served her detention and was riding the late bus home. When she got home, no one else was there yet except for Melanie, who was in the kitchen having a snack. She wondered what the normal routine was. As a secretary, her mother only worked part-time and was home by three, so she was always there when they'd gotten home from school. But as a nurse, Jen had no idea. Since she worked in a doctor's office, her hours should be more regular than if she worked in a hospital, but still, Jen doubted she'd be home for them after school every day.

She joined Melanie in the kitchen and listened to her jabber on about Keaton and Ashley—Keaton swore up and down he didn't like Ashley as anything more than a friend—but Melanie wasn't sure she bought it. Half-listening to Melanie, Jen noticed a schedule posted on the refrigerator. Her mother worked only three days a week at the doctor's office. On two of those nights their father would start dinner, but tonight it was their turn.

"Aren't you going to have a snack?" asked Melanie. "You usually can't wait to raid the refrigerator."

"I really need to watch my calories," said Jen, by reflex.

"Why?" asked Melanie. "You've never worried about it before. You're skinny as a rail. I mean, even considering that everyone wants to be twenty pounds underweight, you're still doing okay."

That's right, Jen thought. When she was in her teens, she never had to worry about her weight.

"You're right," she said, helping herself to an apple from the bowl on the table. An apple was healthy anyway.

They got started on making dinner. As they chopped vegetables, Jen thought about the simple routines of a family, routines she had just assumed she would one day have with her own husband and kids. Suddenly, tears stung her eyes. She tried to keep Melanie from noticing, but it didn't work.

"What's wrong?" Melanie asked. "You're not worried about the detention, are you? Because I don't think you'll really be in trouble. You didn't have to call mom or dad, did you? I won't tell them."

"That's not it." She regarded Melanie. "Do you ever worry maybe you'll never meet the right person and get married and have kids?" She carefully kept the word gender neutral, even though Melanie hadn't realized yet that she preferred girls.

"Well. . ." Melanie seemed taken aback by the question. "I don't even know if I want to get married and have kids. I guess I don't really think about it much." She regarded Jen. "Is *that* why you're crying? Why would you be worrying about that *now*?"

"Uh—I don't know. I—I guess maybe I'm just getting my period or something," Jen stammered.

"Oh. Maybe you need some Advil and chocolate," suggested Melanie.

"Good idea," said Jen, a smile breaking through her tears.

But that's when it hit her. If she stayed in this life, she would have tons of time again. Time to meet the right person. Plenty of time before her eggs got old. Time to get an advanced degree. Time to do things right.

Or screw them up all over again.

Chapter Three

They were interrupted by their father and Ben, who had just come home and burst into the kitchen.

"Hey, how's it going?" their father asked. He enveloped each of his girls in a sideways hug.

"Jen needs Advil and chocolate," Melanie said.

"What?"

"Nothing, Dad, she's just kidding," said Jen, embarrassed. She and her father had always been reasonably close, but not close enough to discuss premenstrual symptoms or cramps. She was surprised Melanie just blurted that out, but then Mel was only eleven. Again.

"I want chocolate!" shouted Ben.

"It's almost dinnertime, buddy," said Dad. "How about if you set the table?" Jen got out a stack of plates from the cupboard, since Ben couldn't reach, and set them on the table so he could put them in the right spots.

"Are you having chocolate, Jen?" Ben asked, unwilling to let the issue drop.

"No one is having chocolate, Ben, I swear." Jen grinned at him. "Mel was just joking."

"Oh, okay," said Ben.

"Maybe after dinner, buddy," their father said.

Ben set the plates around the table. Jen got out glasses, silverware, and napkins.

"You didn't need to get out the silverware." Ben scowled. "I can do that myself. You always just let me do that."

"Oh, sorry," said Jen. "I guess I just wasn't thinking." It was surreal hearing him tell her she "always" did something she knew nothing about.

"Well, I guess it's okay, just this once," grumbled Ben.

"Thanks, big guy." Jen grinned and patted him on the shoulder.

"But next time, let me do it."

"Okay."

Their mother was working late that night, so it was just the four of them for dinner. Again Jen tried to mostly just listen, because she was never sure when she might say something wrong. Her dad asked about her day, which she tried to discuss without encouraging further questions. After dinner and helping out with the dishes, she escaped to her room to do homework.

Eighth-grade homework didn't exactly require total concentration, so she started thinking. She flashed back to her conversation with Melanie. This could be her golden opportunity! She would have a second chance at life. She could apply her thirty-seven-year-old wisdom to choices in what she wanted to study, career, dating, everything.

But having to go through the rest of eighth grade and high school all over again! That would be awful, especially if today was any indication. She supposed she could handle it for a few years, but it wouldn't be much fun. By the time she got to college, it wouldn't be so bad, though. She'd always enjoyed going to school. And then she could study something different, if she wanted. She had to admit, if she were honest with herself, that she was getting burned out on teaching, though she had loved it at first.

But what made her so sure she would even get to do all that? What the hell had happened anyway? She'd been hit by a car and suddenly been thrust into a whole different reality. Who was to say something like that couldn't happen again? And how on earth could she find out? She had learned the hard way that saying the wrong things to the wrong people could have grave consequences and it had nearly cost her her freedom.

***

It wasn't until she was getting ready for bed and cleaning out the pockets of her jeans that she came across Miguel's note again. She wondered why he hadn't mentioned it at lunch. Curious as to what he had written, she unfolded it.

Hey, I don't even know your name yet (he'd written the note before he'd even had the chance to talk to her), *but I think you're really hot. You seem like the type of person who would give a new guy a chance. Text me at (509)555-6374.*

Miguel

For someone who had impressed her as having some depth, especially for a thirteen-year-old boy, the note wasn't exactly poetry. *At least there aren't any spelling errors,* she thought. Not that she would encourage a kid who liked her that way anyway, even if she was one too, at least physically. Emotionally she was still thirty-seven years old, and even the thought of being attracted to someone so young was, well, gross.

He seemed like a sweet kid, though, at least he had when she talked to him today at lunch. She'd have to try not to hurt his feelings.

The next day Miguel didn't try to catch her eye in class, but at lunch he sat with her as he had the previous day. "I was hoping you'd text me last night," he said. He was trying to act nonchalant, but she could tell she'd hurt his feelings.

"Sorry, Miguel," she said. "I didn't get a chance. I wasn't blowing you off or anything." She didn't know what to say. Not the truth, that was for sure.

"Hey, it's cool," he smiled at her. "So I take it you don't have a boyfriend here."

"Nope." She considered telling him she had a soon-to-be ex-husband. She smiled to herself at the thought.

"Hey, I saw that smile. Were you thinking about someone? Do you have a boyfriend back in Seattle, maybe?"

Jen saw an out and leapt on it. "Well. . .yes," she said, smiling shyly and looking down.

"Oh, okay." Miguel looked disappointed. "But it's not like you're married to the guy, right? I mean, he's pretty far away."

Jen shrugged. "Not that far. And we still email and text and talk on the phone all the time."

"Well," said Miguel. "You can still be friends with another guy, can't you?"

"Sure." Jen had to give him credit; he wasn't easily discouraged.

Just then Lucy approached, lunch tray in hand. "Hey," she said, sitting down beside Jen as if they sat together every day. "I'm Lucy," she said, giving Miguel her most flirtatious smile. "You must be Miguel."

"Hey, Lucy," Miguel said, politely but without much interest.

"Lucy's in my art class," said Jen.

"Do you like art, Miguel?" Lucy asked. Lucy's flirtatious tone surprised Jen. It was a departure from her usual sullenness.

"I like art," said Miguel. "But I'm more into sports."

"Were you on any teams at your old school?" Lucy asked.

"Basketball and track."

"It's too late to go out for basketball now here, but you should go out for track," Lucy said enthusiastically.

"I might," said Miguel. "How about you, Jen? Are you into sports?"

"Not really," said Jen, which had always been true.

"Jen's in band." Lucy's voice held just a trace of disdain. Jen wondered how Lucy even knew that. Then she remembered Lucy had seen her with her flute this morning on the bus. At least she remembered to bring it today.

Miguel didn't seem to share Lucy's distaste. "Jen, that's great! What instrument do you play?"

"Flute."

"Really? I play guitar. We should get together and play sometime."

"Sure, maybe," said Jen. She didn't miss Lucy's frustrated expression when the information she used to try to turn Miguel away from Jen had only made him more interested in her. It was all she could do not to laugh, even though it would have been fine with her if Miguel liked Lucy. Jen noted with irony that Miguel was the only male to show any interest in her since Josh. It figured that he'd be seriously underage.

"Why do you think Miguel likes you and not me?" Lucy asked her later in art class.

"I don't know, Lucy; I really don't." Jen remembered the story she had told Miguel. "It's not like I've been trying to get his attention. I have a boyfriend back in Seattle."

"You do? Really? How come you never told me?"

Jen shrugged. "I'm telling you now. We've only known each other for a couple of days." She couldn't believe how easily she'd gotten caught up in middle school drama, despite being more than two decades too old for it.

"Maybe that's it. You haven't been trying to get him to like you," Lucy said thoughtfully.

"Maybe."

"Maybe I should have a party and invite him. That might get his attention. I mean, you won't mind, right, since you have a boyfriend?"

"I wouldn't mind," Jen said. "But I'm not sure if Miguel is really a party sort of guy."

Her motivation for trying to discourage Lucy was actually due her belief that if Lucy had a party, it would be without any adults present.

"You think he wouldn't like a party?"

"Well, he doesn't know anyone here yet," Jen pointed out.

"Then wouldn't he appreciate the opportunity to meet some cool kids?"

Jen shuddered to think of Lucy's definition of cool. She figured Lucy didn't mean cool in the traditional popular sense. "Cool" to Lucy would mean troublemakers.

"Lucy, you wouldn't get a chance to talk to just him," Jen pointed out.

"Who said anything about talking?" Lucy said with a knowing grin. "We could always go to my bedroom to be alone."

Jen hadn't thought her heart could sink any further. Not that anything Lucy said particularly shocked or even surprised her. But how could she talk her out of this?

Without thinking, she struck a low blow. "Do you really want your mother and her loser boyfriend stumbling in on you?"

Lucy's cheeks flamed. "I guess you're right." She turned away from Jen and focused on her artwork.

Jen touched her arm. "Hey, Lucy, I'm sorry I said that. I wasn't trying to be mean or anything."

"No, you're right," Lucy said sharply, loudly enough so that several heads turned in their direction.

"Is everything all right here?" the teacher asked.

"Fine!" Lucy snapped.

"We're fine. Sorry." Jen said.

The teacher moved away. Jen wasn't sure what to say and so didn't say anything. They worked in silence for several minutes. Finally Lucy broke the silence.

"I almost never have anyone over because I never know what I'll find at home," she said.

"I thought you said you had the place to yourself a lot and so you could have friends over whenever you wanted," Jen said.

"I do have the place to myself a lot. I'm just never sure when they're going to come back and embarrass me." Lucy looked near tears as she said this. Jen felt so bad for her.

"Hey, listen," she said to Lucy. "We should get together this weekend. Like maybe go to a movie or something. Maybe I could get Miguel to come too."

"What would your boyfriend think about that?"

"I don't think he'd care as long as you were there, too. As a sort of chaperone." Jen grinned.

Lucy smiled back. When she did, Jen realized how rarely she smiled. That had been true when she was Jen's student as well.

"Maybe we could," Lucy said. She tore a piece of paper from her notebook and wrote down her cell phone number.

***

So that was how it happened that she, Lucy, and Miguel had plans to see a movie on Saturday night. Miguel needed little convincing when she called him later that evening to ask him to go, even when she told him Lucy would be coming along as well. She knew Miguel was hoping she'd change her mind and forget her alleged boyfriend who, after all, lived pretty far away when she couldn't even drive. She felt a little bad about that, but she'd be careful not to lead him to believe they could be more than friends.

During the day on Saturday, she wanted to do something else first. She got permission to take the bus to the mall, saying she needed to get a science magazine so she could review an article.

"Can't you just review one online?" Melanie asked her as she was getting ready to leave.

"Our teacher said it had to be from a print magazine and listed several we could choose from," Jen replied, fudging the truth a little.

"Can I come with you?" Melanie asked next.

"It will be really boring. I'm just going to be looking at science magazines at the bookstore. I'm not going to be shopping for anything fun," Jen said, hoping against hope that Melanie wouldn't persist.

"Couldn't you shop for something fun after that?"

"I know," Jen said. "Why don't you take a later bus and meet me? Then you won't have to be bored while I look through magazines."

She convinced Melanie to meet her in two hours. She figured that should give her time to do what she wanted. Melanie hadn't thought she'd need so long, but when Jen explained it might take a while to find a suitable article, Mel reluctantly agreed.

Rather than taking the bus headed to the mall, Jen took the one headed downtown, where there was a little new age shop where a lady gave Tarot readings in the back. There was a sign-up sheet for the Tarot readings near the cash register. Jen had been a little worried she might have to wait awhile on a Saturday, but the place wasn't crowded. She and Amy had come here once after work to get Tarot readings. Amy liked new-agey things. Today there was a person ahead of her getting a reading, but the saleswoman said she'd be done in about ten minutes.

Jen had been wracking her brain trying to think of whom she could talk to about what had happened to her. Someone who could a) reassure her that she wasn't somehow losing her mind, and b) help her figure out what might happen next. Was she here for good or not? If not, why bother to do anything here?

But where did you go for help when you were transported to some bizarre alternate reality in which you were thirteen years old again? She had no idea. The yellow pages wouldn't be any help. The internet might be if she knew where to start. But whatever help she could get would definitely have to be outside the mainstream. So she decided to start in the only place she could think of. At least the Tarot reader, if nothing else, had an open mind and might be more likely to accept her story than most other people.

While she waited, she looked at the funky jewelry in the shop. She also browsed through the books, but didn't find anything she thought might help her. Finally it was her turn to see Chloe, the Tarot reader.

The little room in the back of the shop where the Tarot readings were done was a testament to stereotypes. Chloe, a slender middle-aged woman with long, dark hair, wore a long, flowing purple caftan. She sat at a table covered with a cloth that matched her attire. The tablecloth wasn't solid purple, however, but purple with gold suns. There was a crystal ball to one side, but Jen supposed this was just for show. Chloe hadn't appeared to have any use for it when Amy and she had been there before. The room was dimly lit, but not so dim that Chloe would be unable to see the Tarot cards. The room and Chloe sort of looked like something Jen might expect to see in a Harry Potter book, and she wondered why Chloe felt the need for such theatre. Jen had gotten psychic readings from other people and most psychics dressed like everyone else and didn't have crystal balls sitting around.

Chloe smiled a welcoming smile when Jen entered the room. "Hi, hon, what brings you here today?" she asked.

One of the many things Jen had noticed over the past few days and was having a hard time getting used to was the way everyone treated her like a kid again. Not that there was anything disrespectful in Chloe's manner. She wouldn't even call it patronizing, exactly. It was just different than how she'd reacted to Amy and her when they'd been there before. Like how you'd talk to someone much younger. She hesitated before entering the room. "I don't know quite where to start, I guess," she said.

"Come on in and have a seat," said Chloe. "It's funny— you're what—fourteen, fifteen?"

"Thirteen," said Jen.

"It's just I have the impression of you as somehow being much older. Something in the way you move, or something like that. I don't know. I can't put my finger on it exactly."

"Well, that's sort of what I wanted to talk to you about," said Jen.

"Really?" Chloe sounded puzzled, but chose not to press the point. She had Jen shuffle the deck and cut the cards. Then she did a layout. "Huh, that's interesting. I'm getting the impression that you see yourself as much older than you actually are as well."

"That's just it. I *am* older."

"What do you mean? I thought you just said you are thirteen."

"I know I look thirteen. And in this—reality, I guess I am. But until just a few days ago, I was living in a totally different— reality. A totally different existence. I was a thirty-seven-year-old teacher and all broken up because I was getting a divorce and time was running out for me to have kids and I was down on myself because I didn't have my master's and my brother and sister have these totally, married with 2.3 kids lifestyles, even my sister, who's a lesbian, for God's sake. Well, they had a commitment ceremony, but still. . ." Jen stopped when the look on Chloe's face finally registered with her.

Chloe was staring at her, slack-jawed. She even looked a little frightened. Jen wondered if Chloe, like her mother, thought Jen was having some sort of psychotic break. She wouldn't blame her if she did think that.

"Does that," Jen said, nodding her head at the card layout, "say I'm crazy?" She tried for a bit of levity.

Chloe studied the cards once more. She appeared to be seriously considering Jen's question. Finally she looked up. "I don't see any mental instability here," she said, relaxing a little and smiling a bit at Jen. "And I don't think you're lying. Actually, I believe you are a very honest person."

"You can tell I'm mentally stable from the cards?" Jen asked skeptically.

"Well, remember, the cards are only a guide. They help me focus my psychic abilities. But from what I can tell, I'm seeing a stable person who has been through quite a bit of grief lately."

"Yes," said Jen. Jen had been reasonably impressed when she and Amy were here before, but it wouldn't exactly take psychic abilities to see the grief when she had just mentioned a divorce.

"When you were talking about your divorce and all that—it didn't sound like a kid playing a trick or something. I mean, I guess a kid could overhear someone saying something like that and then repeat it. But I just got the feeling you had really been in that situation." Chloe was starting to sound a little shaken up again.

"I was—I am," Jen said. "Then a few days ago, I was really upset, crying, and I wasn't paying attention when I crossed the street. I don't remember exactly what happened, but I must have been hit by a car. Everything went black and I felt like I was floating. Then I heard a buzzing sound and realized it must be an alarm clock. And it was, but it was an alarm clock in a room that looked like my room when I was a kid, but updated. And then my sister came into the room, and she was eleven years old again, and . . ." Jen stopped as she became aware that she was babbling again. She hadn't exactly been able to talk to anyone about this for days, and now it was just all pouring out.

"The cards do indicate that you have just made a very long and unusual journey," said Chloe.

"I guess you could say that. I mean, not geographically. I was living here in Riverside before, too. And the year, 2012, was the same, too. But apparently I'm in some alternate—reality—I guess you'd say, in which I'm only thirteen years old in 2012. I guess that's where the unusual part comes in."

"I guess so," said Chloe. She had a faraway expression on her face. She held that expression, saying nothing for so long that Jen finally said, "Chloe?"

"Yes?" Chloe still sounded far away, but she at least seemed to have heard the question.

"Can you tell if I'm here for good?"

Chloe finally seemed to focus on her again. "Do you want to stay here for good?"

"I'm—not sure."

"Really? Because I almost get the sense of—oh, I don't know exactly. Not that you were wasting your life. But almost like you didn't want it anymore. Like you'd made such a mess of it that you just needed to start over."

The words sent chills down Jen's spine. She could feel the color leech from her face. When she met Chloe's eyes, she could barely get the words out. "That's exactly what I said to myself right before I was hit."

Chapter Four

Chloe regarded her for a moment, fascinated. Finally she spoke. "It's as if your saying that to yourself and your emotional state at the time just before you were hit caused some sort of—reaction—like something to do with quantum physics?—in the universe, so row, you've gotten what you wished for, the chance to start over."

Huh? Jen thought, her mind reeling. "What are you talking about? Quantum physics?"

Chloe's face clouded over. "I don't know," she explained apologetically. She smiled. "Sometimes things just come to me that I don't really understand.

"So, Jen, now you've got the chance to start over. You're thirteen years old again. You have your whole life in front of you. You can make completely different choices. Get that graduate degree. Don't marry the guy who's wrong for you. Actually, I don't suppose you'll meet that particular one at all here. But you can use the wisdom from the life you left behind to keep you from making bad choices in this one."

"I know. Believe me, I've thought of that. Part of me is really psyched about the possibilities."

"But you're conflicted."

"Well, yeah. Thirteen is a horrible age to go back to," Jen said. "Middle school has been awful. Who wants to go back and take PE and try and fit in among middle-schoolers again?"

"That will only be for a little while though, right? Thirteen is what, eighth grade?"

"Yeah, but I don't imagine high school would be much more fun. It's not just that, though. In fact, that's not the real problem at all. I'm sure I could handle a few difficult years."

"Then what is the real problem?" Chloe asked.

"Well, I don't know what happened to cause my—reality—or whatever you want to call it—to change. I don't know if I'm here for good or not. If not, nothing I do here will matter."

"If you don't think anything you do here will matter, why did you bother going to school at all? You could play hooky every day, do whatever you wanted."

"Well, my first day here, I figured I was either in a coma or dead. So I said some things to my mom, about how I was really thirty-seven years old and none of this was real and other things, and she freaked out and brought me to the emergency room; she thought I had completely flipped out, and I narrowly avoided becoming an inpatient on the adolescent psych ward. So I figure I should at least play along for now."

"Yeah, I can understand that," said Chloe.

"But I'm still not sure if I'm here for good or what."

Chloe didn't speak for several minutes, concentrating. Finally she said, "I don't think you'll be pulled away from here suddenly."

"You mentioned a physics connection earlier," Jen said. "I know you don't really know anything about quantum physics, but is there a way you can tell me anything more about the connection of physics to my situation?"

"Well, let me see . . .here in the layout we see the Hierophant, which can represent a clergyman, but I think in this case it's a teacher or mentor. I see the physics connection attached to him somehow."

"So, a teacher who could help me figure out what happened, maybe?"

"Yeah, maybe."

"I don't know if an eighth-grade science teacher would be able to provide much help in quantum physics," Jen mused. "It's not exactly an area of focus that he would have to keep up on for his students. A physics professor at the university, maybe?"

"I definitely think that's a possibility," said Chloe enthusiastically. "You should check that out.

"I should tell you though," Chloe continued. "If you do connect up with this teacher or mentor or whatever, you may end up having to make a difficult choice."

"You mean, stay here or go back to my old life?"

"Exactly."

***

Once outside, Jen glanced at her watch. She had a block to walk to the bus stop. The bus would arrive in about ten minutes, which was perfect. When she got to the mall, she would just have time to buy a magazine and then meet Melanie.

As she walked along, she realized she felt strangely relieved, probably because she had finally been able to unburden herself to someone. Plus, talking to someone at the university was a good idea. At least she had a tentative plan of action.

The bus made several stops before arriving at the mall. She'd only been in this new reality since Monday, but she missed driving. When she finally got there, she headed straight for Barnes and Nobles. She didn't have much time before she had to meet Melanie, and she didn't want to not have the magazine when she should have had plenty of time, so she grabbed the first decent science magazine she saw. She paid for the magazine and hurried to the prearranged meeting spot, where Melanie already sat on a bench, waiting.

"Geez, took you long enough," said Melanie.

"Sorry," said Jen, out of breath from practically running. She took a closer look at Melanie. Beneath the scowl she saw Melanie was near tears. "What's wrong?" she asked.

A single tear slid down Melanie's cheek. "Keaton broke up with me," she said.

Jen sat down on the bench and put her arm around her. "Oh, honey, I'm sorry."

Melanie shrank away. "Don't say it like you're soooo much older and wiser! It's not like you've had a lot of boyfriends either!"

"No, I guess I haven't," said Jen, though she had no idea how many she'd had in this reality. "But I *am* sorry," said Jen.

"Thanks," said Melanie.

They sat in silence for a few minutes. Then Jen remembered something that had always cheered Melanie up before. "Do you want to get some ice cream?"

Melanie brightened a bit. "Sure," she said.

They headed toward Baskin-Robbins, where they both got hot fudge sundaes with World-Class Chocolate Ice Cream. They were just sitting down to eat when Jen's purse buzzed. Pulling out her phone, she saw she had a text.

It was from Lucy: *Sorry can't go tonight.*

Alarmed, Jen replied immediately. *What? U can't cancel! The whole point of this was so Miguel could get to know u!* If Jen went with Miguel by herself, he might get the wrong idea. She had to get Lucy to change her mind.

Her phone buzzed again. *"He likes u anyway. Dump Seattle guy n go out with Miguel.*

Lucy, I can't go out with Miguel. I don't like him the way he likes me!

By now Melanie had picked up on her state of mind. "Who are you texting?" she asked, trying to read the texts over Jen's shoulder.

Jen tried to block her view. "Stop being nosy," she said, to little effect.

Another buzz. *UR mentally ill.*

"Maybe, but why are u bailing? Is everything OK?"

Yes, sorry, got to go, bye. Jen felt far from reassured.

"What's wrong?" Melanie asked. "And who is Miguel? Your boyfriend? Does mom know?"

"Calm down, " said Jen. "And you really shouldn't read other people's texts. Miguel is just a guy from school. I only like him as a friend. I'm supposed to go to the movies with him and my friend Lucy tonight, but Lucy just backed out."

"So it's just you and Miguel?"

"Yeah, and I don't want him to get the wrong idea." Then Jen thought of a solution. "I know—why don't you come with us?"

"Oh yeah, he'll really appreciate having your little sister along if he likes you," Melanie retorted.

"He wasn't expecting to be alone with me. Lucy was supposed to come, remember? And I told him I have a boyfriend back in Seattle."

"You have a boyfriend in Seattle and didn't tell me?" Melanie asked indignantly.

"No—I made that up so I wouldn't hurt his feelings. I just want to be friends."

"Oh—okay."

"So—don't blow my cover. If you want to come, that is."

"Okay, I guess."

*   *   *

"So who is this boy?" their mother asked later at dinner. Jen nearly burst out laughing. Her mother hadn't much cared for Josh, but before she got married—finally, according to her mother—she had always been inquiring about Jen's love life. Now, though, her mother greeted the possibility of romance in Jen's life with deep suspicion.

"He's just a friend, mom," Jen said. "My friend Lucy was supposed to come, too. But she backed out, and that's why I want Melanie to come with us. So he doesn't get the wrong idea."

"Well, I guess it's okay then."

"So can you drop us off?"

"Sure."

She and Melanie got there a bit early. They got sodas and popcorn and sat at a table in front of the snack bar where they could watch for Miguel. Jen waved when she saw him. He smiled and waved back.

"That's Miguel?" Melanie asked.

"Yeah."

"And you just want to be friends?"

"Yeah."

"You *are* mentally ill."

"Well, maybe."

Melanie laughed. Jen had told Melanie what Lucy had said, and apparently Mel agreed with Lucy.

Miguel paid for his ticket and sauntered over to them. "Where's Lucy?" he asked.

"She called this afternoon and told me she couldn't make it. This is my little sister, Melanie."

"Hey Melanie," he said, smiling at her.

Melanie smiled brilliantly back at him. "Hi."

"So are you the chaperone then?" he asked with a grin.

"I guess so." Melanie's smile grew uncertain.

Miguel got his own snacks, and they went into the theater. Jen sat in between Melanie and Miguel. The movie was funny, geared toward the teen set, but not too bad. She'd had to remember not to choose something rated R, a struggle given the possible choices. She got the uncomfortable feeling that Miguel wanted to hold her hand, but he didn't try to do so. She was glad Melanie had agreed to come along. She wondered what happened to Lucy. Jen hoped she was okay.

After the movie ended, they waited outside together for their prospective rides. Miguel asked Jen about Lucy. "So why did Lucy bail?"

"I don't know why Lucy couldn't come," said Jen. "She texted me this afternoon and said she'd have to cancel. I hope she's okay."

"Me too," said Miguel. He hadn't shown much interest in Lucy one way or another up until this point, but now he seemed concerned. Good, Jen thought. Maybe she could get him interested in Lucy rather than her. But would that be such a good idea? Would he be a good influence or would Lucy be a bad influence? Not that Lucy was a horrible kid, but her home life was so unstable, and she did tend to get involved in things she shouldn't. And while Miguel didn't seem that easy to influence, she didn't know him well enough to be sure.

Just then their mother drove up. They said good-bye to Miguel. Their mother asked if he needed a ride, but he said no, his own mother would be there soon. Jen thought again about how she missed driving herself.

"How was the movie?" their mother asked.

"Good," said Melanie.

"It was okay," said Jen.

"That was a good-looking guy there," said their mother. "Are you sure he isn't your boyfriend?"

"Yes, I'm sure." Jen blushed.

"Because I know you'll be getting into the dating thing again," said their mother. "And after that whole debacle in Seattle. . ."

What debacle in Seattle? A date rape? A pregnancy scare? Had she been dating a drug dealer, maybe? She couldn't very well ask. Melanie's comment earlier, asking if she had a boyfriend without telling her, suggested that Jen had not had a boyfriend there, at least not right before they left. But obviously something major had happened.

"Don't worry, mom," said Jen. "Miguel is just a friend. I swear. I told you, that's why I wanted to bring Melanie along."

"I was the chaperone," Melanie said brightly.

"Well . . . OK then." Their mother didn't sound entirely convinced.

"Mom, what do you think they were going to do, make out right in front of me?" Melanie asked.

"Mel! Not helpful!" Jen said sharply.

"Well, you wouldn't."

"True. But it wasn't necessary to be quite so—descriptive."

"Sorry," said Melanie, not altogether sincerely. Jen had the distinct feeling the whole conversation both fascinated and amused her.

"Sure you are," said Jen.

"I am!"

"All right, girls, that's enough," their mother said.

Jen's cheeks flushed with embarrassment. In the space of a few days she'd regressed to adolescent squabbling with her sister.

"Sorry, mom," she said.

"Me, too," Melanie said.

Jen was wondering how she could get them to tell her what happened in Seattle without revealing that she didn't know when Melanie provided a clue.

"Anyway, Miguel seems really nice," Melanie said. "Not like Roger."

Jen assumed Roger was the guy back in Seattle with whom the "debacle" had occurred.

"Well, Jen thought Roger was nice at first, too," their mother said.

"Yeah, but she met him online. Not at school. It's easier to lie about yourself online," Melanie pointed out.

"That's true," their mother agreed.

So Roger was some jerk she'd met online. Jen wondered why her mother allowed her to keep a computer in her bedroom if she worried about her meeting guys online.

"And as I said, Miguel is just a friend." Jen's voice had a slight edge to it. She was annoyed that her mother didn't seem to be quite convinced Miguel was just a friend—as if she would bring Melanie along if she had been interested in anything more. It also annoyed her that the conversation involved a whole series of events she knew nothing about and couldn't ask about without arousing suspicion.

"Mom, you can trust me," she said, trying to sound reassuring and not like an irritable adolescent.

"I know, Jen," her mom said. "I wouldn't let you keep a computer in your room if I didn't trust you. And as Melanie rather bluntly put it, you wouldn't have brought her along if you were planning to do anything besides see a movie with Miguel. I'm just being a worried mom."

"It's okay, mom." To her surprise, Jen's irritability vanished. Instead, she felt touched by her mom's concern.

"It is?" Her mom seemed startled. "Usually you get mad at me when I act like a worried mom."

"Well—let's just say I'm having an unusually mature moment," said Jen.

"Okay—I guess I'll enjoy it while it lasts," her mother said, laughing. After that, the conversation petered out. Jen wondered again what happened in Seattle. She had a little more information—she met some jerk named Roger online who lied about himself—but what exactly had happened? For her mother to classify this as a fiasco, something must have happened beyond online chats. She must have at least met him.

She supposed it didn't matter what happened. Still, she couldn't help but be curious and if her family was going to bring it up, she wanted to have at least some idea of what they were talking about. She wished she could just ask, but her mom and Melanie would think she was nuts. Maybe she could think of a way to get Melanie to talk about it later without it seeming like she didn't know what happened.

She had another idea. As a teenager in the 80s, she'd kept journals. She decided when she got home, she'd search her room to see if she had any handwritten journals. She'd check her computer as well to see if maybe she had a journal on there. She had not thought to look for a journal until now, but it could be interesting to see what her teenage alter-ego had written.

When they did get home, Jen was glad Melanie didn't seem to want to hang out with her. Probably she had her own friends to text or chat with. Jen had searched her room pretty thoroughly the first day she'd been dropped into this new existence, trying to find clues about her new life, but now she did so again. No handwritten journal. So she turned to her computer. Looking through the "My Documents" folder, she didn't see any obvious possibilities for a document that might be a journal right away. She hadn't labeled anything "journal" or "diary". Most things looked like school assignments or downloads from the internet.

She was starting to feel discouraged, but she didn't want to give up too easily. She realized she might have used a misleading name for the file, in case Melanie or her parents came snooping. With that thought, she decided to open each file and look at it. Even if she didn't find a journal, just seeing the files on her computer could help her learn more about her alter-ego.

Most of the files *were* school assignments, and uninteresting to read through. Nor did they yield much useful information. How bizarre to think of some alternate version of herself living in the same times, but a different world. Someone who'd written all these reports. It looked as if she was a decent student, at least, as she had been in the 80s as well.

Hours had passed since she first started searching. Her mother tapped on her door—Jen didn't have a specific bedtime anymore, but her mom wondered if she planned to go to bed anytime soon. Jen assured her she would and got ready for bed, turning out her overhead light, but then she got back on the computer. She was ready to give up when finally she opened a document entitled "Washington History Paper" and hit pay dirt.

She had indeed done what she'd thought she might have. Her parents or perhaps more importantly, Melanie, would never think to look here. This was a journal she'd started in the middle of seventh grade. She hadn't written too often, maybe once or twice a week. She skimmed through the entries, figuring she could read more carefully later. Many weren't that interesting; they were just complaining about school assignments or her parents or siblings getting on her nerves. She'd written about her friends and hated her looks and wondered if she'd ever get a boyfriend.

The millennial Jen wasn't that different from the Gen-X Jen at age thirteen, at least not if this journal was any indication. Having much more technology at her disposal seemed to be the primary difference. Jen felt vaguely disappointed. She'd hoped the millennial alter-ego would be more interesting.

Around six months ago, shortly before they'd moved away from Seattle, she'd apparently gone on a social networking site for teens and met a kid named Roger who claimed to be thirteen, also from Seattle. Jen was certain she had found true love. She'd written numerous journal entries gushing over him, such as this one:

September 13, 2011

Roger is awesome. I can't believe I have so much in common with him. We like the same music, the same movies, and the same foods. We like the same subjects in school even. His profile pic is HOT!!! Kenetia and Morgan and all my other friends agree. We are supposed to meet next week at a football game between our two schools.

Meeting at the football game was innocuous enough. Middle school football games were during the day, right after school, and there would be other people around. Jen had talked to him on the phone before meeting him, but other than thinking he sounded "more mature" than thirteen or fourteen, their conversations hadn't set off any warning bells in her naïve alter-ego's head.

September 17, 2011

Roger didn't show up at the football game. I was so disappointed, and embarrassed. I was there with all my friends who were expecting to meet him, and he didn't show. I just wanted to go home. But Kenetia and Morgan talked me into staying, saying he was a jerk, and probably that wasn't even his picture on his profile. So I stayed, and halfway through the game, he sent a

*text. I called him back, and he apologized. He said he chickened
out, and he felt shy meeting me at the game when he knew my
friends would all be there, and could we please meet somewhere
where it could be just us? I told him I would meet him at the mall
about halfway between his school and mine on Monday after
school, and I wouldn't bring my friends with me.*

Well, at least she had still proposed meeting him at a public
place. But it must have gotten worse here somewhere, especially
since it sounded as though her parents had been unaware of any of
this.

Several days passed before she'd written another entry. And
it was a doozy.

September 23, 2011

*I finally met Roger a few days ago. I couldn't wait. I knew I
was about to meet my soul mate. I could see us staying together all
through high school and going to college together and then getting
married. Morgan and Kenetia thought I shouldn't get my hopes up,
since he'd already canceled on me once. Plus, who stays with their
first boyfriend forever? But I figured just because they hadn't met
the right person—just because people usually don't meet their soul
mate so young, didn't mean I hadn't.*

*Morgan and Kenetia understood why he might not want to
meet me with all my friends hanging around, but they thought they
should come to the mall with me, just in case he turned out to be a
real jerk. They thought they could arrange to run into us at a
certain time and make it seem random. I thought that would be
okay. I would tell them we should go see a movie that weekend if I
needed them to somehow ease me out of the situation with Roger.
So we all went to the mall after school. I went to meet Roger. I was
supposed to suggest we get some ice cream at Baskin-Robbins,
where Morgan and Kenetia would already be eating. I said what if
Roger didn't want ice cream. They just said try to talk him into it
or at least guide him in that direction. If we didn't show up in
twenty minutes or so they would call me on my cell and I'd tell*

them where I was, acting like I was talking to my mother, and they would "accidentally" bump into me a few minutes later.

This was getting way too complicated.

Waiting for Roger, I was really nervous. Morgan and Kenetia told me I looked great, that he would totally love me. I wasn't so sure. I wore a new outfit and had taken some extra time with my hair and makeup in the girls' room after school, but I would have bet such a good looking guy (if his picture could be believed) would have no trouble getting a girlfriend much prettier than I am. But I successfully fought the urge to bolt, and he showed up at our meeting place a few minutes after I got there.

He looked GREAT. Even better than his picture, and I didn't think that was possible. He had a terrific smile, and he was soooo nice. He took my hand and told me how great it was to finally meet in person, and he was glad I understood about his no-show the other day. I said not to worry about it. I asked if we could get some ice cream. He said sure. So we walked over to Baskin-Robbins, where Morgan and Kenetia were waiting and trying to act like they weren't. They had wasted no time in stuffing their faces, in any case. I think his hotness stunned them. I deliberately steered him away as quickly as possible. I didn't say anything about wanting to see a movie that weekend.

We went up to the counter and ordered some ice cream. When we had gotten our orders and sat down—Morgan and Kenetia still across the room, stealing glances at us—I asked, "Are you really only thirteen?" I couldn't believe we could be the same age. He looked so much older.

He flushed and looked away. Then he looked back and said, "No, I'm really sixteen. I know I shouldn't have said I was only thirteen, but I was afraid you wouldn't talk to me if I told you my real age."

I figured this explained why he avoided video chatting. His profile picture was probably taken when he was younger.

I should have seen that for what it was—a red flag. Lying, for one thing. And what sixteen-year-old wants to hang out with a thirteen-year-old?

One who wants an easy victim, that's who.

But at the time my head was swimming with infatuation and I didn't care. I accepted his explanation. We finished our ice cream and walked around the mall for awhile, holding hands the whole time. We played some video games in the arcade for awhile. Then Roger asked if I wanted to go for a ride.

Even though he had said he was sixteen, I hadn't thought about how that would mean he probably had a driver's license. I felt a little scared at the thought of going for a ride with him, but a little thrilled. too. "Just a short ride," he promised.

So we went out to his car. Little did I know Kenetia and Morgan were following us some distance behind. They were impressed with how hot he was, but worried about how much older he looked. Especially Kenetia, because her older sister was date-raped last year. They saw us get into the car, and Kenetia wrote down the license plate number.

I was still in seventh heaven. Roger was so wonderful, and he had an awesome car with a great stereo. We just drove around and talked for a long time. He put his hand on my thigh from time to time. It made me a little nervous, but I didn't exactly hate it, either. I didn't start to feel like something was wrong until I realized we had been gone a long time and we were in an area of Seattle I didn't recognize, pretty far away from the mall.

"I think maybe we should go back now," I said. I had told my parents I was going to the mall after school with Kenetia and Morgan. They weren't expecting me home until dinnertime, but that would be soon, and I still had to catch the bus from the mall and get back home.

"Aw, come on." Roger flashed me a dazzling smile. "You don't really need to go yet, do you?"

"Yes, I really do," I said. "I told my parents I was at the mall with my friends and that I'd be back in time for dinner."

Roger abruptly pulled the car over, at which point I noticed we were in an isolated area. I wasn't sure where, but it was by a cemetery, very creepy, especially since the day was overcast and it was starting to get dark.

"I told you, you don't need to go home yet," Roger sounded angry. I was really scared now. He suddenly seemed completely different, like not such a nice guy. He grabbed my arm and pulled me toward him. I tried to pull it away but couldn't. He yanked me toward him, toward the space between our seats, and hurled me into the back seat. I scrambled for the lock, but it was one of those child-proof ones I couldn't unlock. Frantically I reached into my jacket pocket for my cell phone—couldn't think what else to do but dial 911—but then he was in the back seat beside me. He wrapped his arms tightly around me, pinning my arms to my sides. He kissed me then, shoving his tongue in my mouth, which gave me the opportunity to bite it as hard as I could. He shrieked and pulled away. "Bitch!" he screamed. He smacked me in the face, but his grip on my other arm had loosened, so I tried to get to my cell phone again. That's when we heard the sirens. Lights flashed in the rear window. Every Lifetime movie I'd ever seen (my favorite station) flashed through my head.

"Shit!" Roger shouted. He let go of me and vaulted into the front seat. Would he try to get away from the police or something? It was too late, though. The cruiser pulled up behind us before Roger could even get the car started.

It turned out there was a warrant out for Roger's arrest in Oregon. I hadn't even noticed the Oregon plates on his car, but Kenetia and Morgan had noticed. They had briefly argued over what to do when they saw us get into the car and got the license plate. Morgan thought it was uncool to rat me out to my parents, but Kenetia had prevailed because Roger looked so much older and because of what had happened to her sister. So they called my parents, who called the police. They told the police everything Kenetia told them, that I had met this guy over the internet, he was several years older, I had gone off in a car with him, and I might be in danger. They ran the plates and that's when they found out about the arrest warrant. Roger wasn't even his real name. It was Evan Steed, and he was wanted for sexual assaulting a fourteen-year-old in Portland, whom he had also met on the internet. Well, my parents and Kenetia and Morgan were freaking out. No one knew exactly where we had gone, but Kenetia told my parents, who told the police, which direction we had gone from the mall. We wouldn't have been found so quickly, though, if there hadn't been a cruiser already in the general area, checking out a vandalism report.

So the police officer cuffed Roger/Evan and took us both to the police station, where my parents picked me up. Evan was transported back to Oregon, where I guess he'll go to juvy.

I've never been so embarrassed to face my parents! Of all the ways I had imagined this evening's ending, having my parents pick me up at the police station was not even in the top thousand. Though I admit I was glad to see them, even as embarrassed as I was. I could barely even look at them, and as soon as I did, I burst into tears. "I'm sorry," I said. I could hardly speak, I was crying so hard.

My mother went into nurse mode. "Honey, what happened, did he hurt you?"

She accidentally gripped my arm in the same spot where Evan had gripped it, though not as hard. "Ouch!" I said. The pain had ironically cut through the crying jag. "He didn't hurt me like you're thinking. He grabbed my arm right where you grabbed it and he hit me here." I indicated my left cheekbone and eye area.

"You might get a black eye," she said, inspecting it.

"If I do, can I stay home from school tomorrow?" I asked. "I don't want to go looking like that."

"We'll probably have you stay home anyway," she said. "You've just been through a horrible experience. You should

probably rest. Right now I want to take you to the emergency room to get checked out, just to make sure you're okay."

I hated that idea.

"Mom, I'm okay, really," I said, but there was no arguing with her. You'd think since she's a nurse she'd just trust her own medical judgment, but if anything, her medical knowledge tends to make her more likely to haul me into the doctor's office rather than less.

The ER doctor told us the same thing she had—that I'd probably have a black eye and some facial swelling. The doctor asked if she needed to do an internal exam—I swore up and down she didn't. I didn't think the doctor believed me at first, but my clothes weren't torn or anything, and my mother said she believed me. The doctor . . .

There was more—much more. But Jen couldn't read any more. It was the strangest experience to read about someone who was supposedly her, yet not her. Discombobulating. Of course she didn't remember any of these events, and yet. . . she had the strangest feeling of recognition, of deja vu. It was almost as if the journal was a book she had read before, one whose character she identified with more than most. Odd, to say the least. But the surreal feeling had worn her out and it was almost two in the morning. She dragged herself to bed.

Chapter Five

Her mother woke Jen late the next morning. "Jen, are you ever getting up?" she called, knocking lightly on Jen's door.

Jen fixed one bleary eye on her clock. 10:57. She couldn't believe she'd slept so late. "Give me a few minutes," she mumbled. She'd been having strange dreams about what she'd read last night in her journal. About Evan. And this morning, the journal's contents felt more like—memories—of events that happened to her rather than something she'd read.

She had only been here a few days, but it seemed much longer than that. And every day, this reality seemed a little more real, while her previous life, the one she considered her "real" life, seemed more and more distant. Reading the journal and her subsequent dreams raised another disturbing possibility. Was she in danger of losing her past as well as her present? Was that what this do-over would cost her? Nothing made any sense.

Jen's mother knocked on her door again. "Brunch is in five minutes," she said.

Well, as long as she could remember her past—her eighties childhood in Montana, her teaching career, her divorce, her family and friends as they were in her old life— she wouldn't lose it. But here, she had no one with whom she could share her history. No one except Chloe so far, that is.

As if to counter the point, Aquarius jumped up on the bed beside her. "Why are you here with me now?" Jen asked as she stroked the purring cat. Aquarius' presence here with her made no sense. Not that anything else about the situation made sense either. "Do you remember Josh?" she asked the cat, as if Aquarius could answer. The cat regarded her. Something knowing in the cat's stare almost made Jen wonder if this Aquarius *could* remember Josh and their life before.

"I'll be right down," Jen called out. She stroked the cat again. "I'm glad you're here with me, whatever the reason."

She hauled herself out of bed and pulled on a pair of sweats and a T-shirt. Boy, it was nice to have someone else cook. Josh hadn't been too helpful in that regard, and before she had gotten married and after Josh had left, it had been kind of a pain to cook for one person. The smell of bacon and hash browns made her stomach growl.

Later, stuffed with pancakes, bacon, eggs, and hash browns, she first did her math homework, then read a short story for English. Then she thumbed through the science magazine she had bought the previous day. She could summarize almost any article, so she searched for a good one. She didn't find anything interesting to her until she happened upon an article about Hugh Everett.

The name meant nothing to her, but he was apparently important in the physics world. Since Chloe had mentioned physics, she decided to read on about his contributions in that area. Jen didn't care much about the original question Everett had been trying to answer, which was why quantum matter behaves erratically. However, she found his Many-Worlds Interpretation fascinating. According to the theory, any time an event had more than one possible outcome, the universe split into different universes for each possible outcome. So, for example, the universe had split when she made the decision to marry Josh. Sure, she had thought herself in love, but she'd had her doubts. She chose to marry him because she feared she might not meet anyone else before time ran out for her to have children. And according to the Many-Worlds Interpretation, the universe had then split into two separate universes, and in one of those she hadn't married Josh.

Too bad I couldn't just get into that universe somehow, she thought. But did the theory have something to do with her current situation? She couldn't shake the feeling that somehow it did, even though she couldn't see how. How could she have made a decision that had caused her to be 24 years younger but still in 2012? It made no sense.

Would anyone at the university know about this kind of thing? She got on the computer and found the university's website.

Once there, she clicked on the link for the physics department. There she scrolled through brief bios for each of the faculty members, looking to see if anyone studied quantum physics. The university in Riverside only had a small physics department. As she scrolled through the names and read through their research interests, disappointment filled her as she realized none seemed to include quantum physics. She was starting to think no one at the university studied it until she scrolled to the bottom. There she found Dr. Elwood Murphy, Professor Emeritus, whose main research interests included the applications of quantum mechanics. She hesitated. Dr. Murphy would almost certainly think she was nuts, but she needed some answers. If he thought she was nuts or a kid with an extremely active imagination, so be it. She clicked on the "contact" button and began composing an email. After several false starts, she decided, screw the truth. The most important thing was to get an appointment to see the professor. She could be more honest in person, when hopefully he'd be less apt to dismiss her as a crackpot. It would be too easy for him to do that in an email.

Dear Dr. Murphy:

I am a high school junior who is interested in quantum physics. I am starting to research colleges and I am impressed with your research in the area of applications of quantum mechanics. [In truth, she'd only scanned a list of his published articles, but she hoped the ego-stroking would be enough]. *I was wondering if you'd be willing to meet with me briefly to discuss the physics department at WSU-Riverside.*

Sincerely,

Jennifer Edwards

She hesitated only a moment before clicking on SEND.

Now what? She hated waiting for people to answer emails, and he probably wouldn't respond until at least tomorrow, since it was Sunday. She finished her summary of the article on Hugh Everett and tried not to think about it.

After maybe half an hour, her email notification sounded. The professor had answered her already!

Dear Ms. Edwards:

If quantum physics is truly your interest, this university may not be the best place for you. I'm the only one here who specializes in that area. I do still teach a couple of classes covering such topics as string theory and the Many Worlds Interpretation, but I think you might be happier at one of the many universities where much cutting-edge research is being done in this area. However, if you are from around here and economic circumstances dictate that you attend college close to home for a couple of years, you could at least get some basic requirements completed. In any case, I'd be happy to speak with you. Would Monday at four work for you?

Sincerely,

Dr. Elwood Murphy

Jen was surprised to be able to see him so soon. Let's see, she thought. School got out at 2:30. It was so annoying not to be able to drive. She perused the city bus schedules she had picked up a few days earlier. If she got on the number 52 bus at the stop one block from the school at 2:45. . . it took her a couple of false starts, but finally she figured out she could take that bus to the mall, transfer to the number 10 bus, and get to the university by 3:40. She then went to WSU-Riverside's website again and printed out a map of the campus. She tucked that and the bus schedules into her binder.

Now she had to think of an excuse for tomorrow. Where could she say she needed to go? It had to be something her parents wouldn't mind her doing, but that wouldn't lead to Melanie's asking to tag along. She couldn't say she had plans with Lucy, because Lucy rode the same school bus as she and Melanie did. Melanie would see Lucy on it tomorrow and know Jen was lying. Maybe she could say she wanted to go somewhere with another friend? She supposed she would have to say that. Her parents would know she didn't have a doctor or dentist appointment. The problem was, Melanie might see her walking to the city bus stop alone. The school bus drove right past it, and Jen would have to walk past the area where the school buses waited for the students to get to the city bus stop. She would have to think of a good cover story which would allow for that possibility.

She emailed Dr. Murphy back, telling him she would see him Monday at four. She had thought of a story that should work; she would ask permission at dinner.

At dinner she listened to Ben and Melanie chatter on about nothing in particular. Her mom told a funny story about something that happened at work the previous day. Jen couldn't help but notice how much happier she seemed as a nurse than she had as a secretary.

After her mother finished her story, Jen took advantage of the pause in conversation.

"I've made a new friend in the last few days at school," she said. "Her name is Katie, and her aunt is in town tomorrow. Katie is taking part of the school day off to spend time with her, but she asked if I could take the bus to the mall after school and meet them there. Would that be okay?"

"Well, sure, I guess," her mother said. "Are you sure it's all right with her aunt for her to have a friend along?"

"Oh, yeah," said Jen. "Her aunt told her she wanted to meet some of her friends, and she has the early part of the afternoon to be alone with Katie."

"Well, I'm glad you're making some friends at school," said her mom. "I know it's taken awhile and it was hard to leave Seattle."

"How come you never told me about Katie?" Melanie asked suspiciously.

"Well, it's only in the last few days that we've really become good friends," said Jen. "Before that, we'd just talk in class and stuff."

"Whatever." Melanie pouted. Jen supposed Melanie's reaction was better than simple disbelief.

"Melanie, it's just there was nothing to tell."

"Mel, Jen can't be expected to tell you every little thing," their father pointed out.

"I guess," said Melanie, somewhat mollified.

"So is it okay?" Jen asked, just to make sure.

"Yes, it's okay," her mom said. "Do you know what bus to ride?"

"Yes, I already figured it out," Jen said. "It's pretty easy. All I have to do is get on the number 52 bus at the stop one block from school at 2:45. It goes straight to the mall." Of course, she left out the fact that the mall was not her final destination.

"Okay then."

***

Morning arrived way too early for Jen. She was tempted to fake illness, despite the potential difficulty of fooling her mother, the nurse. But then she remembered her appointment with Dr. Murphy after school today. She couldn't very well go to that if she stayed home "sick" today.

So she hauled herself out of bed and dragged herself through her morning routine. On the bus, she sat next to a sulky Lucy. Jen figured she probably wouldn't say much this morning in a mood like that, but she did ask how Jen's evening with Miguel had gone. Jen told her about it.

"Why did you bring your sister with you?" Lucy wanted to know.

"Because I just want to be friends with Miguel. I didn't want him to get the wrong idea."

"You're crazy." Lucy said, turning toward the window.

"What's wrong with you this morning?" Jen asked her.

"Nothing!" Lucy insisted. She refused to say more on the subject, but Jen still thought something had happened at home over the weekend to upset Lucy. Something that still upset her. Jen just hoped whatever happened was magnified by adolescent angst and not anything serious. Lucy's mother's boyfriend still worried Jen.

Jen barely paid attention in class. Luckily no one called on her and caught her off guard. In school now she did more cooperative work in groups than she had as a teenager in the 80s, so she couldn't always just sit and pretend to be listening. So when she had to work in groups, she participated just enough so the other group members wouldn't complain.

In art class Lucy was still distant. Jen tried to figure out how to get to the bottom of it without annoying Lucy to the point of Lucy refusing to talk to her at all, which, knowing Lucy, could happen. Finally she just asked, "Did I do something to make you mad?"

Lucy's demeanor thawed slightly. "No, it's not you, Jen. I'm sorry I bailed on Saturday night."

"I'm not worried about Saturday night. But can't you tell me what's wrong? I mean, we're friends, right?"

"Girls, are you getting any work done?" their art teacher interrupted.

"Sorry," Jen said.

"Let's do less talking and more working." The art teacher circulated away from them.

Jen and Lucy worked on their projects in silence for several minutes. Then Jen said, "Well?"

"Well what?"

"Well, aren't we friends who can tell each other things?"

Lucy sighed. "Jen, seriously, why do you want to be my friend?" A couple of kids at other tables glanced her way, so she lowered her voice. "You aren't anything like me."

"What do you mean?" Jen asked, though she had a feeling she knew what Lucy meant.

"Oh, come on," Lucy scoffed. "Like you don't know what I mean. You're in all the advanced classes, you don't get into trouble like I do, I'll bet from your clothes that your parents have quite a bit more money than my mom does, and I'll bet you don't ever have to worry about not being able to get a ride somewhere because your parents are passed out drunk!"

Lucy spoke in a near whisper, but intense enough that several students looked over at them until the bell ringing distracted them.

"Lucy, I'm sorry," Jen said. "I didn't know what happened. But why didn't you tell me? We could have given you a ride."

"You think I wanted you to see that? If your parents knew what my family is like, they probably wouldn't even let you be my friend."

Jen figured this might be true. They both finished cleaning up and stood to go.

"You know, it's weird," said Lucy, as they left the classroom. "But you don't even seem like someone our age. You make me think of a counselor or someone. No, you know who you remind me of? This teacher I talked to last year when my parents were getting divorced. She was always asking me how I felt and shit like that."

The words hit Jen like a bolt of lightning.

"What teacher?" she asked, hoping her voice didn't betray her astonishment. Obviously it couldn't have been her, but in this world, someone must have taken up the slack.

"Mrs Jensen, my seventh-grade language-arts teacher. She noticed my grades dropping and I wasn't turning things in. She kept making my mom come in for conferences and all that. I had to see the counselor all the time too, because this teacher made a counselor referral. But it's like you could be her daughter or something."

A shiver ran down Jen's spine. "I'm sorry if I annoyed you." She tried to keep the quaver out of her voice.

"Don't worry about it. It's just I don't want to be counseled."

"Okay."

Lucy regarded her. "Are you okay? You look like you've seen a ghost."

"Yeah, I'm fine." Relieved Lucy's irritation seemed to have passed but shaken up nonetheless, she said goodbye to Lucy and raced toward her next class, leaving before Lucy could ask her anything else.

Lucy seemed to be the only one, except Chloe, who could see that while she appeared to be a thirteen-year-old girl, on the inside she was much older.

But of course, Lucy had met someone much like Jen, someone who had served her role in Lucy's life here.

Someone who also had the married name Mrs. Jensen.

At the end of the day, she ran upstairs to the seventh-grade hallway. She hadn't been up here since—well, in this universe. She headed toward the room that was her classroom in her old life. The name outside the door did say "Mrs. Jensen." The door was closed, but the light was still on. Cautiously she eased the door open.

The teacher was in the middle of a phone conversation on her cell. "Josh, I don't know why you're arguing with me about a cat," she said. "I'm done talking to you. Goodbye." She pressed the END button and set the phone down on her desk. Then she looked up and saw Jen standing in the doorway.

"Yes?" she said. "Can I help you with something?"

Fortunately, Jen was leaning against the door frame. Otherwise she might have fallen over. The resemblance between her adult self and this woman was that striking. When Jen didn't say anything right away, Mrs. Jensen stared at her, starting to look a bit annoyed. "Can I help you with something?" she asked again.

"Sorry." Jen struggled to explain her presence. "My friend thought she left her binder here, but I don't see it."

The teacher cast her eyes around the room. "No, I don't see it either."

"Thanks," Jen said. "We'll check the lost and found."

"Is that it then?" Mrs. Jensen asked, when Jen didn't move right away.

"Yes, except—sorry for eavesdropping, but—Josh sounds like a real jerk. I'm sure you'll find someone much better."

The teacher looked stunned. Then she smiled at Jen, saying, "I hope you're right."

Chapter Six

Jen walked to the city bus stop in a daze over her surreal encounter with the teacher. That combined with her nervousness over her upcoming appointment was giving her a slight case of vertigo. She had no idea what she would say to the professor. She thought about it as she walked to the bus stop and then on the ride over. She had hoped she might think of something to say last night, but she hadn't been able to come up with anything other than a few questions about the physics department in keeping with her cover story. And frankly, she figured she might not even need those, because she doubted the professor would buy the cover story as soon as he saw her. Maybe he would think she was a young-looking high school junior, but maybe not. While she thought her appearance was somewhat improved from her first pass through adolescence (at least partly because mullets were out of fashion), she didn't think she looked particularly old for thirteen.

She supposed she'd just have to wing it. She pulled her campus map from her backpack. Geez, could the physics building *be* any further from the bus stop? When she finally got there, she had only a few minutes to spare. She reached into her backpack for a water bottle as she hurried across campus. Her throat had gone dry from nerves.

She found a directory just inside the physics building. The professor's office was on the third floor. Jen took the elevator; with her lingering vertigo she thought she might pass out if she tried to walk up three flights of stairs.

A young college student with long brown hair smiled at Jen as she stepped into the elevator. Jen smiled back nervously. The button for the third floor was already lit up. Both she and the girl got off there.

"Are you going to see Dr. Murphy too?" the girl asked Jen, after they'd gone down the hall a short distance and it became rather obvious they had the same destination in mind.

"Yeah," said Jen, unnerved. She was anxious enough without this girl right on her heels.

"My name's Taryn Westlake," the girl said. "Are you a student here? I don't think I've seen you around before."

"I'm Jennifer Edwards, but you can call me Jen. And no, I'm not a student here. I'm still a junior in high school, but I might go to college here."

"I thought you looked kind of young—" Jen paled slightly when Taryn said that—"but I wasn't sure. Anyway, this isn't the best place to go for physics. The department isn't that big and they don't specialize in what I'm interested in. And I should warn you," she lowered her voice as she continued, "Dr. Murphy is pretty eccentric. But he's been great to work with, even though he's pretty weird. And by going to school here I can live at home for a couple of years and save money. I can get my basic courses done and then transfer to a university with a bigger physics department."

"Yes, that's what I was thinking, too, about living at home for a couple of years first," said Jen, relaxing slightly. "So what kind of physics are you interested in? And what do you mean, eccentric?"

"Well, I think you'll just have to meet him to see what I mean," said Taryn, still keeping her voice down. "But he's harmless, so don't worry. As for what I'm interested in, it's the far-out stuff that I'm into. Quantum physics, especially the Many-Worlds Interpretation, things like that."

"Me too!" Jen said excitedly. But even in her excitement, she couldn't help but think it was truly a parallel universe if she was contemplating studying physics, even as a ruse.

"Did you have an appointment? I just need to ask him a quick question," said Taryn.

"Yes, I have an appointment at four, but go ahead and ask your question," said Jen. "I'm not in a hurry."

"Great, thanks! Hey, I'll be in the café in the student union next door if you want to talk afterwards."

"Sure, that would be great!" Jen said. Maybe it would be helpful to talk to Taryn. It sounded like she knew something about parallel universes.

They had reached the door Jen presumed was Dr. Murphy's, but Taryn didn't knock. She just walked right in. "This is the lab," she explained. "We have to go through it to get to Dr. Murphy's office."

Complicated equations and diagrams covered a large whiteboard on one wall. A large white screen dominated another wall. There were six large tables, mostly covered with equipment like lenses, cables, computers, and other equipment Jen couldn't identify.

"Is this a classroom?" Jen asked. With all the tables, it looked like it, but to her it seemed messy for a classroom.

"Dr. Murphy has classes in here sometimes, and sometimes he just does his own research in here."

"Is it just his lab? I mean, does he share it with anyone?"

"It's just his. He has family money, which basically paid for this building. It's not a big building, but you may have noticed it's pretty nice, new and updated and all that."

Jen had noticed.

"Anyway, he got the best space. The university seems to regard him as some sort of mad scientist, but they put up with him because of his money. Also, he published quite a bit when he was younger, but not as much recently."

They reached a closed door at the other end of the room, and this time, Taryn did knock.

"Come in!" an older man's voice called.

Taryn opened the door and charged into the room, Jen trailing after her. "Hi, Dr. Murphy," Taryn said. "This is Jen. She has an appointment with you at four o'clock?"

The professor's appearance astonished Jen. She hadn't expected a professor emeritus to be young, but this wizened man looked to be in his eighties, at least. His attire made her wonder if he was color blind, or if he just liked loud colors. He wore a bright purple shirt with orange and green plaid pants. Large glasses dominated his face. He was a diminutive man, but what he lacked in height and stature he made up for in hair—it was big, wild, and white. It reminded her a little of Christopher Lloyd's hair in *Back to the Future*.

"Hi, Dr. Murphy, I'm Jennifer Edwards," she said hesitantly, extending her hand for him to shake.

"My, you look young." Dr. Murphy's strong grip surprised Jen, and his voice, now that she wasn't hearing it from behind a closed door, also sounded stronger than his frail appearance would suggest. Jen flinched at his words, but Dr. Murphy continued. "Of course, the students appear younger to me every day."

He looked over at Taryn. "Are you just the welcoming committee, or did you need to talk to me too?"

"Just a quick question, Dr. Murphy. Did you get any potential research assistants for me to interview tomorrow?"

"A couple. Here are their names—wait, where did I put that note?—oh, here it is." He handed Taryn a slip of paper.

"Thanks," said Taryn, taking the paper. "I guess I'll see you tomorrow then."

Once Taryn left, Jen felt a flash of panic, as if Taryn had been protecting her in some way. But before she could decide how to start the conversation, the professor started talking.

"You do look young—are you sure you're a junior in high school?" he asked with a smile.

"I'm older than I look," Jen said, smiling back. It was the absolute truth.

"So what got you interested in quantum physics?" he asked.

"Well—" she decided on the fly to stick as closely to the truth as possible here—"I honestly hadn't given any branch of physics much thought until I started reading about Hugh Everett and the Many Worlds Interpretation." She hoped he wouldn't ask too much about the physics she had studied in school. Except for the little bit she had studied recently in her 8th-grade science class, she wouldn't be able to recall much.

"It's a fascinating theory," the professor agreed, his gaze intent. "Did you know I went to graduate school with Hugh Everett at Princeton?"

"No, I didn't know that," Jen said.

"He left the field of physics after he got his PhD," said Dr. Murphy. "His Many Worlds Interpretation wasn't well received at the time. In fact, it was met with scorn. But it's gotten much more favorable attention since then. Personally, though I kept my feelings to myself at the time, I thought and still think the idea has merit, though it does have disturbing implications."

"Like what?"

"Well—it sounds like you know the basics of the Many Worlds Interpretation," he said, and when she nodded, he continued. "Say there's a situation in which there could have been two outcomes, one of which would have been your death. According to this theory, the universe would split at this point, and in one of those universes, you would be dead."

Jen shivered, wondering if this was in fact the case for her, that she was dead in some other universe, since she'd been hit by a car. After all, at first she'd figured she was dead or in a coma in the only universe she knew.

She hesitated a moment before posing her next question.

"Dr, Murphy, have you ever heard of anyone—traveling— to a different universe? Like involuntarily?"

"What are you talking about?" Dr. Murphy looked confused now.

"Would it be theoretically possible for someone to travel between parallel universes? Or to somehow get sent to another universe?"

Dr. Murphy still looked mystified. "Not according to the Many Worlds Interpretation. Parallel universes never come into contact with each other." He regarded her. "May I ask why you're asking?"

He'd probably just think she was nuts, but she decided to go for it. "Dr. Murphy, I have to be honest. I came to see you under false pretenses. I'm not a high school junior. In this— universe—I'm only thirteen. That's why I look so young. But in another universe I was a 37-year-old Language Arts teacher who grew up in Montana. I'm now a student in the school where I taught! It's crazy! I was just living my life, and one day, I was hit by a car. I felt like I was floating in blackness for a long time. Then I woke up in a totally different reality, one where my family is much younger—I still have the same parents and siblings, only my brother and sister and I are growing up in 2012 rather than the 80s. And my cat—that's the weirdest part. Well, it's all weird, but I have this cat, Aquarius, and she's been with me in both of these realities. . ." Jen's voice trailed off as she noted the professor's reaction to her story.

He was just gaping at her, stunned.

"Dr. Murphy?" Jen asked hesitantly when he didn't speak for what seemed like an eternity.

"It's finally happened," he said, as he shifted his gaze away from her and at some point over her shoulder.

"What's happened?"

"I've lost my mind," he cried. He looked as if he truly believed it. "I guess I should have fully retired last year. Because now my mind has snapped!"

Alarmed, Jen rushed to reassure him. "No, you haven't lost your mind, Dr. Murphy. I just told you a very bizarre story, that's all."

"Did you tell me you've come here from another universe? Did I hear you correctly?"

"Yes, Dr. Murphy, you did. I was. . ."

"Young lady, is this some kind of joke?" Dr. Murphy sounded angry now, like he might be about ready to demand she leave his office. She couldn't let that happen. Not yet.

"Of course not," Jen cried. "How could I even think of such a bizarre story if it weren't true? And why would I come here and hassle someone I've never even met? I can tell you all kinds of details from my childhood in Montana if that will help." She was talking quickly so he wouldn't interrupt. She wasn't sure if this would help—maybe he would just think she got the details from someone older and was just repeating them, but she had to try to get him to listen to as much of her story as possible. She rushed on.

"My parents were two of the first people I knew of to get a cell phone. It came with a huge battery pack that was almost like a briefcase or even small suitcase. I'll bet almost no one today could even tell you about those, because hardly anyone owned one then. People didn't even really call it a 'cell phone' then. They said 'cellular phone' or 'car phone'—"

"There must be pictures of those old cell phones on the Internet."

"Why would I even think to make up some little detail like that just to support some crazy-ass story? I remember records and eight-track tapes. I never owned any eight-track tapes, just cassettes, but my dad had eight-tracks, at least he did when I was little, in the seventies. My parents had a stereo where you could stack a bunch of records at once and it would drop down one at a time. I got one of those when I was ten, but theirs also had an eight-track player. I owned a bunch of 45s; my favorite singers were Duran Duran, Rick Springfield, and the Go-Gos. My favorite movie from the 80s is *Back to the Future*. Of course I could have seen that anytime, but I saw it in the theaters in 1985. I LOVED Michael J. Fox; I never missed *Family Ties*. I remember when the Challenger blew up in 1986. I was home from school, sick, that day. . ." she trailed off, trying to gauge Dr. Murphy's reaction.

He looked thunderstruck.

He stared at her for several minutes without speaking.

When he did speak, he said, "You could have heard or read all that somewhere. Maybe you did some kind of report on the 1980s or something for school."

"Well, I didn't. Before I came here, I was going through a divorce. My married last name was Jensen. When I started attending Riverside Middle School as a student, I realized the teacher in the room I had in my original world also had the name Jensen. She married Josh—my soon to be ex—in this world. They're getting divorced too. Josh was trying to get custody of my cat, ridiculously enough, and I overheard this teacher arguing with him on the phone about a cat as well!"

Dr. Murphy gaped at her again for a long moment. Jen was surprised his jaw hadn't actually hit the floor. Finally he spoke. "Probably not too many thirteen-year-olds—or anyone, really— would think of making up a story such as this. And . . .you just sound like an adult somehow. . .but this is impossible. . ."

"So, is there any theoretical explanation for what's happened to me?"

"It's true that in the Many Worlds Interpretation the universes can't come into contact with each other," said Dr. Murphy. "But the Many Worlds Interpretation isn't the only one that proposes parallel universes. And in some other theories, parallel universes can interact."

"I was just wondering if I would be staying here or end up back in my old life just as suddenly as I ended up here."

"Well, I just don't know; I'm sorry to say." The professor did appear regretful. "There are all sorts of theories in speculative physics about parallel universes and the multiverse. But this—this is from science fiction."

"Before my accident, I was thinking about how much I just wanted a do-over. I was getting a divorce, my ex was fighting me for custody of my *cat*, I had gotten in trouble at my job, and things just weren't going well."

"So it's as if you got your wish," the professor said in a contemplative tone, staring off into space.

"Maybe I should have been more specific, though. Middle school has NOT been fun, and I'm sure I wouldn't enjoy high school any more the second time around than I did the first. Why couldn't I have gone back to age twenty-one or so? And there's something else I don't understand."

"What's that?"

"Well, I know there's more than one theory that allows for the possibility of parallel universes. And if the Many Worlds Interpretation is correct, anytime you make a decision in which more than one outcome is possible, the universe branches off, correct?"

"Yes."

"But how could I have made a decision that would have made me twenty-four years younger in 2012?"

"Well, it probably wasn't your decision," the professor said, looking fascinated. "Probably it was decisions other people made."

"Such as?"

"Such as maybe your grandparents on both sides in this world made decisions that caused them to meet and get together and have kids a few years later than they did in your world. So then both your parents would have been younger, and maybe then they waited a little longer to have kids in this world. . ."

"I guess something like that could have happened," Jen said. "But still, twenty-four years is a huge difference."

"Well, but it could have started back earlier than your grandparents even. Maybe even a couple of generations or more before them. Little decisions people made or things that happened could have been magnified over time."

"Yeah, I guess that could have happened. Plus, I think here my parents did wait a little longer to have kids than they did in my—I never know what to call it—real life. They both seem a little older than they did when I was thirteen the first time. Not much. Like maybe five years or so.

"I just wish I understood how I got here," Jen continued. "You really have no idea?"

"It's as if somehow you went through a wormhole, but I don't see how you could have."

"A wormhole?"

"Haven't you ever watched *Star Trek: Deep Space Nine?*"

"No."

"Oh. Well, anyway, it just connects two distant regions of space, a shortcut, if you will; the characters on the show used to use them all the time. Some scientists—like Stephen Hawking— propose an infinite number of parallel universes connected by wormholes. And there could be a way to travel through those wormholes that we just haven't figured out yet. I just can't understand how you seem to have done so by accident. I wish I had a better answer for you. Some theorists do think time travel will eventually be possible through these wormholes. Can you believe that?"

"Yes. I'd believe anything at this point," Jen said dryly. "But—I guess I don't understand how parallel universes and time travel are related."

"Parallel universes take care of the grandfather paradox, the paradox of time travel!" the professor exclaimed, as if it were obvious. "Say, for example, you traveled back in time to your grandparents' childhood. What if you killed one of them at a young age? Then you'd never be born, but if you were never born, how could you have killed one of them?"

"So if there are parallel universes, the universe just branches off, right? Another universe develops in which the killer is never born."

"Exactly!" The professor said, beaming at her as if she were his star student.

"But I guess it still doesn't make sense to me," Jen said. "I mean, if you killed your grandmother when she was little, a parallel universe could branch off from there in which you were never born. But in one universe, your grandmother would still have been killed as a little girl by someone who wouldn't have been born if she hadn't been alive to give birth to the parent of her killer."

"What?" the professor asked, confused.

"Exactly!" Jen exclaimed.

"It is pretty complicated," the professor admitted.

"I must say," Dr. Murphy said as she was leaving, "you've made my day. It appears that travel between universes is at least possible."

"Sure, involuntary travel," said Jen.

"But that's better than not being possible at all!"

"I guess," said Jen.

" And if you were able to do it involuntarily, it must be possible to do so on purpose. And in that case, time travel is probably possible!"

"That would be pretty exciting," Jen admitted. "Sometimes I've wished I could travel back to a time right before I made a really big mistake. Sort of like 'System Restore' on the computer."

"Haven't we all wished for that?" the professor agreed.

"I have one more question," said Jen. "Why did my cat come to this universe with me? I mean, I didn't have a cat growing up, but I had one as an adult, and I have one here, now. It seems to be the same cat. She looks the same and responds to the same name and seems to have the same personality."

"I don't know what to tell you about that," the professor said. "But then the whole thing is pretty bizarre. I think maybe the cat was just destined to be with you no matter what."

Chapter Seven

Jen's visit with the professor had taken longer than she realized. It was almost five. The last bus she could take left at 6:30, which she guessed would be all right. She'd told her mother she might have dinner with "Katie" and her aunt, but she was supposed to call home if she decided to do that. She still wanted to meet with Taryn and hoped she hadn't left the student union yet. Jen wandered over there and found the café without too much difficulty. Glancing in the window, she spotted Taryn at a table by herself, studying. Good.

She fished her cell phone from a side pocket in her backpack. When she'd found it and happened to glance toward the window again, Taryn looked up also and caught her eye and waved. Jen waved back and then pointed to her phone, holding up one finger to indicate she'd only be a minute. Taryn nodded and returned to her text.

After speaking briefly with her mother, Jen entered the cafe and joined Taryn.

"How was your visit with Dr. Murphy?" Taryn inquired.

"Different. It's kind of a long story. I need to get something to eat first if that's okay. Do you have anyplace you have to be?" Jen had decided to level with Taryn. If Taryn was into quantum physics, she might accept Jen's story as the professor had, albeit with a considerable amount of convincing. Taryn might even have some ideas on what had happened, since she did research in that area.

"No, go ahead."

Jen went to the counter and ordered a burger and fries and soda. She'd been eating a lot healthier in this new reality, since she hadn't been cooking for herself or ordering fast food. So right now she was craving some junk.

Taryn looked up from her textbook as soon as Jen sat back down again. "So what happened that was so different? Dr. Murphy's totally weird, isn't he?"

Jen laughed. Dr. Murphy's weirdness was the tip of the iceberg. "Well, I guess he's a little weird. But what I had to tell him was even weirder."

Taryn looked confused. "Weren't you just asking him about the physics department here?"

"Well, no. I—had a sort of personal—situation that I hoped Dr. Murphy could help me with."

Now Taryn looked even more puzzled. "Um, Dr. Murphy isn't the sort of person one usually seeks out for help with personal issues."

"No, I would imagine not, but I have an unusual—situation, and I needed his expertise."

"You have a personal situation that involves quantum physics?"

"Well, I think so, yeah."

Taryn continued to look puzzled, but then her expression cleared. "Oh, I get it. You like a guy who's into physics. Wasn't this pretty drastic, though? Couldn't you just have read up on some things online—"

"It's not a guy. Listen, I'll tell you my story, but you have to promise me you'll keep an open mind."

"Okay." Taryn regarded Jen with interest now. "So you're not really looking into coming to school here?"

"No," Jen admitted.

"That's too bad." Taryn looked disappointed. "I guess you probably wouldn't have started here until after I was already gone anyway, though."

Jen took a deep breath and started talking. Like Dr. Murphy, Taryn initially expressed disbelief.

"So, let me get this straight. You told Dr. Murphy that you are a thirty-seven-year-old schoolteacher who got hit by a car and somehow got transported into a parallel universe in which it's the same year—2012—but you are only thirteen years old? And he believed you?"

"Well, not at first. He thought he must have lost his mind and started talking about retirement and how he should have done so sooner and—"

"Yeah, I'll bet. Is this some kind of joke? Did you cook this up between the two of you or something?" Taryn sounded almost angry.

"No, no," Jen said. "Who would even think of such a joke? I mean, the professor's weird, but have you ever known him to play a joke like this?" She prayed to God Taryn would say no. "And I swear I've never even met him before today. I sent him an email, saying I wanted to talk to him about the physics department. I lied so he would agree to meet with me, but then I told him the truth today."

"So did you get him to believe you? How?"

"I managed to convince him I'd grown up in the 80s rather than in the new millennium. I gave him examples of things from my childhood, and told him a few things about my adult life. Also, as I pointed out to you, who would even think of such a joke?"

"True." Taryn looked thoughtful. "I don't even think Dr. Murphy would think of playing such a joke, different as he is. And now that I'm talking to you more, you seem older, somehow, though you look young. I thought you looked younger than sixteen or seventeen when I first saw you, but you seemed mature, so I didn't think too much of it." She paused. "But this is so unbelievable!"

"I know. I couldn't believe it myself at first. I thought I must be dead."

"Tell me more about your 80s childhood. Forgive me, but I'm having a little trouble accepting your story. If I had some more details about your—well, your first childhood, maybe I'd find it a little easier to accept, the way Dr. Murphy did. I don't know how else to do this."

"Well, you could ask about my divorce," Jen pointed out. "Or my college days at the University of Montana in the late 80s and early 90s."

"You went to the University of Montana? Not such a great place for physics."

"I studied education and psychology. I'm a teacher, remember? Or at least I was. The wanting to study physics was just a cover story."

"Oh, right." Taryn paused. "So you really are divorced?"

Jen nodded. "I was in the process of getting divorced."

"It's weird to hear someone who looks and sounds so young talk about her divorce," Taryn said.

"Yeah, but what's even weirder is going through the divorce, hating life, wishing you could start all over, then getting hit by a car and waking up twenty-four years younger."

Taryn gasped. "So it's like you got your wish."

"Yeah, but I guess now I have mixed feelings about it. I mean, on the one hand, I get my do-over. But I do wish I hadn't gone back to age thirteen. I guess I should have been more specific in my wish. Do you know what it's like trying to go through middle school again?"

"True." Taryn shuddered at the thought. "So is there a certain age you would like to have gone back to?"

"I don't know," said Jen, somewhat surprised by the question. "I just—I wanted to have certain things done by my age, you know? Or maybe you don't know yet, since you're what, nineteen?"

"I just turned twenty," Taryn said.

"Well anyway, I wanted to have kids, and I got married at thirty-five, thinking Josh—my husband—and I could get started right away before I got too much older. Josh wasn't quite as enthusiastic as I was about having kids, but at least seemed willing, and I knew he'd be a great dad. I thought he was just a little nervous. Now I see how deluded I was. Right after we got married I found out he didn't want kids at all. I was so angry he hadn't told me before we got married. But, stupidly, I still hoped I could change his mind. I wasn't quite ready to admit I had made a mistake. Then I caught him cheating on me, and I had to face facts."

"You actually—caught him at it?" Taryn asked, looking disgusted.

"Yeah."

"That's awful," said Taryn.

"Yeah, and so I started divorce proceedings right away. And I realized I'd wasted even more time by not facing the truth. I was so depressed. I didn't have a husband anymore. I didn't have the kids I wanted, and money was tight with having to pay my divorce lawyer and everything. I wished I'd gotten my master's—no one goes into education to get rich, but if I had my master's I could have at least been earning more, which Josh always liked to point out to me. I just—I just wanted more time."

"I guess that makes sense," Taryn said. "I'm so sorry."

"Thanks. But as you said, I guess I got my wish."

"So why did you go to see Dr. Murphy, exactly?"

"Well, I wondered if he could explain to me how I got here," Jen said.

"Does it matter though?" Taryn asked. "You're here now."

"Well, but I arrived here suddenly, without warning. People don't usually get hit by a car and end up in another universe. So couldn't I end up going back to where I came from just as suddenly? And that would make anything I do here irrelevant."

"And if you stay," said Taryn thoughtfully. "Wouldn't everything you did before be irrelevant?"

It was a troubling question for Jen, one that threatened to send her straight into an existential crisis. "Well, I guess that's both true and not true. I mean, the experiences I had before still affect me now and affect what I do, so in that sense whatever happened in the universe where I was an adult is still relevant. But . . . " she paused.

"But what?" Taryn prompted, when Jen didn't speak again for several minutes.

"But . . . well, it's only been a few days, but it's lonely," Jen said. "I can't talk to anyone about anything that happened in my life or things I did before I got here. I tried at first, with my mother, because I didn't think any of this could be real. She thought I was nuts, of course, and I almost ended up on an adolescent psych ward. So basically any identity I had before a few days ago has been erased. And . . . is a do-over worth it?"

"Boy, I don't know," said Taryn. She was silent for a moment. Then she said, "You mentioned your mother, and the way you were talking about her—do you have the same mother here or something? How can that be?"

"I have the same family here as before," Jen explained. "Same parents, same siblings, except there are more years between my brother and me in this universe than in my original one. My sister is still two years younger here. Everyone was just born later."

"Wow," said Taryn. "So, is your family a lot different than they were in the 80s?"

"It's weird—some things are different and some things are the same. In the 80s, my mom was a secretary, and the job didn't fulfill her. I don't think she was ever happy in that job. In this universe, she's a nurse. So it's still a stereotypically 'woman's' job, but she got a college education, and the job seems to suit her much better. She seems happier. My dad is still a teacher, but we lived in Seattle until recently, where he had a job in a private school that had to close when it went bankrupt. Melanie, my sister, seems much the same as she did when we grew up in the 80s. Just sort of an updated version of the kid she was then. With my brother, it's weird, because he was only four years younger than me in my old universe and he's seven years younger than me in this one. I haven't spent that much time with him, but he's a great kid. The relationship is different since there are more years between us. It makes me realize. . ." Jen trailed off.

"Realize what?"

"Well, I guess it makes me realize how much I miss them. I see them on holidays, and I always visit my parents—well, now just my mom—for a couple of weeks in the summer, but we all live in different cities now. I hardly ever see my nieces and nephew, usually just at Christmas. But anyway, Ben and Melanie are busy with their own families—"

"So, I take it they're both married with kids and everything?"

"Pretty much. Ben is sort of Mr. Perfect. I don't mean to sound snide or like—I don't know, sour grapes or something. Because he really is a nice guy. But he's got the perfect job, wife, house, two kids, one boy and one girl."

"What about your sister?"

"Well, she's a lesbian, so she's not legally married to her partner, but they're more or less a lesbian version of the All-American family. She and her partner have been together for ten years, and they have a daughter who is three. Melanie gave birth to her through artificial insemination. They got a gay guy they know to be the donor. They live in Portland."

"So you're the only one without kids." Taryn said. "That must be tough. I mean, if you didn't want kids it wouldn't matter, but since you do. . ."

"Yeah." Jen realized she was near tears. "I guess maybe it doesn't matter now anyway though. I mean, I have loads of time if I stay here."

"True," Taryn said. "That's partly why you wanted the do-over, right?"

"Well, that, and I wished I'd gotten my master's degree. I couldn't afford to go back to school thanks to the divorce. And I was tired of teaching and starting to wonder why I'd chosen it in the first place, though I loved it in the beginning."

"So did you teach here in Riverside?"

"Yes, that's one of the crazier parts of this whole experience. I'm a student at Riverside Middle School. That's where I taught. My teacher for my language arts/history block was my best friend. She gave me detention on my first day of classes for swearing!"

"You're kidding!" Taryn burst into laughter.

"No!" Jen laughed with her. "I mean, it is sort of funny. I was thinking that she'd be in *so much trouble* if things ever returned to normal, but then I wondered how the hell I could explain to her *why* she was in trouble." She laughed again. It all *did* seem pretty funny now, though she'd been pissed off at the time. Taryn laughed with her.

"Here's something even weirder though," Jen continued. "I went to see who's teaching in the classroom I taught in. It's a woman named Mrs. Jensen. That was my married name! And I heard her talking on the phone to someone named Josh! She even looks like me, and they were arguing over a cat, which Josh and I had been doing the day before I got hit by the car."

"This is just unbelievable. And you say your cat came here with you to this new reality?"

"Yes. I mean, it's not like we traveled together that I'm aware of, but I'm sure it's the same cat. I didn't have a cat growing up, and she looks and behaves just like my cat that I had before."

"The cat you were fighting so hard to keep. Didn't you say your ex was trying to take her away?"

"Yes, the asshole." Jen was silent for a moment. Suddenly she realized they'd been sitting there for quite awhile and glanced at her watch. "Oh, no," she cried.

"What's wrong?" Taryn asked.

"It's 6:35! The last bus left at 6:30. How am I going to get home? Jen tore open her backpack and fished out her wallet. Looking inside, it was as she figured. Not nearly enough for a taxi.

"Let me give you a ride."

"I'd hate to have you go to any trouble," Jen said, but she hoped Taryn wouldn't mind. She didn't want to have to call her parents for a ride and try to explain what she was doing at the university.

"It's not a problem, really. You're so interesting to talk to," said Taryn.

"I can imagine," Jen said dryly. "It's such a pain to not have a driver's license."

"I would HATE that. And having your parents tell you what to do all over again."

"Well, it hasn't been too bad. At least they aren't the hovering types, and they both work and everything." Jen paused. "Even though I didn't want to go back to age thirteen specifically, I had been feeling I'd made such a mess of my life, maybe it's kind of a relief to not be responsible for too much. I just have to go to school, do my homework and some chores, and not antagonize my siblings—which is much easier now than the first time around." She hadn't realized how she felt until she said it. She had been too busy being alarmed by the dramatic turn of events. But she realized there was some truth to this. This—exile—was a break from her problematic life. Even if it turned out to be nothing else.

***

On the ride home, Taryn peppered her with more questions about how her family here compared with the one she'd grown up with in the 80s. She asked about how the school in this universe compared with the one where she taught. She also had questions about the details surrounding Jen's accident, trying to make sense of the situation, but seemed just as perplexed as Jen. She promised to keep thinking about it, and they exchanged email addresses and phone numbers.

"Call or text me on my cell," Jen said as they pulled up in front of her house. "So I won't have to explain to my parents who you are. Or emailing is fine, too."

"Great. And you feel free to get in touch with me anytime, too," Taryn said. "I do hope things work out for you—somehow."

Jen laughed. "Thanks, me too."

***

"Hi, Jen. Did you have fun with Katie?" her mother called from the kitchen as Jen entered the house.

It took Jen a moment to process her mother's words and remember her cover story. "Yes, Katie and I had a great time. Her aunt is cool."

"Oh, good, I'm glad," her mom said.

"Do you want some help with the dishes?" Jen asked. She hoped her mother would say no, though Jen and Melanie normally helped with the dishes after dinner, because she didn't want to answer a lot of questions about her afternoon. She didn't want to have to keep lying.

"No, honey, we're almost done anyway. Why don't you get started on your homework?"

"Okay." Jen raced upstairs. It was funny. She'd pretty much trudged everywhere in her previous life, but now she pretty much moved around like a thirteen-year-old. Of course, it helped that she had less weight to carry around. And it was *sweet* to have her thirteen-year-old metabolism back.

Chapter Eight

Jen hit the snooze button on her alarm. She wasn't up for middle school today. She just wanted to go back to sleep, but any notion of doing so shattered when Melanie burst into her room.

"Why aren't you up yet?" Melanie demanded.

Jen groaned. Why did Melanie have to be such a morning person? She'd forgotten this lovely little attribute.

"You're going to be late!" Melanie prodded.

"I'm sick!" Jen lied.

"Really?" Melanie eyed her skeptically. "You know mom will figure it out if you're faking."

"Melanie, would you please just worry about yourself and go away?" Melanie's hurt look made Jen realize she had gone too far. "Sorry," she said. "I'm just grouchy. Honestly, I don't know why you even want to talk to me first thing in the morning. I'm never in a good mood."

"Guess you're not a morning person," Melanie agreed, and Jen laughed. She had a sense of deja vu, since she now remembered they'd talked about this in her previous life on several occasions.

At least no matter what happened, she still had her family.

Still, facing middle school was never a cheery prospect. Lucy was absent from the bus that morning, so Jen sat alone. She didn't mind that, but having lunch with just Miguel was a little awkward without Lucy there to help carry the conversation. Jen was preoccupied and Miguel kept trying to draw her out.

"Is something wrong? You're so quiet," he said.

'No, I'm sorry," Jen said. "I'm just distracted today, I guess."

"How's—what's his name—Elijah?"

Jen figured he was hoping they'd broken up or something and that was the reason for her distraction. She figured she'd better get that idea out of his head, so she smiled. "Elijah is just great."

"Damn." He grinned to show he was kidding, though she knew he wasn't.

"Miguel—" she began.

"No, really, it's cool," he said, smiling again at her.

Jen had an idle thought. She was an adult in a parallel universe somewhere out there.

What if Miguel was too? What if they were both adults in that same parallel universe? Then they could be together.

"Do you ever wonder about parallel universes?" she asked Miguel.

"What?"

"Parallel universes. You know, universes that exist alongside ours. Maybe one where there's another version of you and me."

"Like in science fiction?"

"Yeah, maybe." Or science fact.

"I don't know." Miguel was looking at her strangely now. "I guess I've read some books that had parallel universes. I like to read sci-fi sometimes. Why?"

"Oh, I don't know," Jen said. "I guess it's just something I think about sometimes. Like maybe somewhere you and I are in another universe, and we're already grown up, like in college maybe."

"Is Elijah in this universe?" Miguel asked.

Jen smiled. "Well, I don't know."

"Let's say he isn't."

Jen laughed. "Okay."

"So we could go out, then."

"Yeah, I guess we could."

"That would be awesome!" Miguel said. "How can we get to this universe? It sounds way better than the one we're in." He laughed.

I don't know, getting hit by a car, maybe? Jen thought. The bell rang, signaling the lunch period's end and saving her from having to answer.

"I hope I don't have to wait until we're old for you to break up with Elijah," Miguel said as they left the cafeteria.

Jen laughed. "College age isn't exactly old. And anyway, we were saying he didn't even exist, in this parallel universe. Not that I broke up with him."

"Couldn't you just *pretend* he doesn't exist?"

Jen smiled. "Sorry, but I can't."

"Damn," Miguel said. A teacher overheard and said, "Language!"

"Sorry," Miguel said quickly.

Once they had passed the teacher, Jen said, "At least he didn't give you detention, like Ms. Whiteside gave me when I swore."

"You swore in class?" Miguel sounded shocked.

"It was right after class." Jen decided not to mention that it was his note to her that had led to her swearing in the first place.

"Still, I didn't think you would do that."

"Well, I did," Jen said.

"Lucy seems to think you're such a goody-goody," Miguel observed.

"Mostly, she's right."

"Oh, I don't know," Miguel said. "I mean, you don't seem like you get in trouble a lot, but you seem different from the other kids, somehow. More like you're into doing your own thing, not going along with the other kids or making teachers happy."

Jen was impressed with Miguel's powers of observation.

"Yeah, I guess you're right," she said.

"See, I'm the same way," he said. "That's why I hope you'll break up with Elijah. Or at least tell him you don't want to be so serious right now."

"I know we're young, but I'm just not interested in anyone else that way," Jen said.

She knew she had to keep up the charade or risk giving Miguel false hope. "Look, can't we just hang out as friends?"

"I guess." Miguel didn't look too happy about that.

"Look, like you said, we're thirteen. Who knows what will happen down the road?" She hoped he would take this as a reason to cheer up without reading too much into it.

"I guess," he said again, without looking at her. Jen sighed. She didn't know what else to say. Fortunately by then they had reached their classroom. They took their seats without saying anything else to each other. Lunchtime went much better with Lucy to act as a buffer, Jen reflected.

It pained her that Miguel was upset, even though she hadn't done anything wrong in just wanting to be friends. And it wasn't as though she could be honest in telling him why.

If Jen went back to her old life somehow, would the person who had been living this life come back here? If so, would that Jen want to go out with Miguel? It would make sense, she thought. Jen had thought more than once that she would have liked Miguel a lot when she was really thirteen herself. For this reason, she felt compelled to try not to mess things up for the other Jen, just in case.

She felt much better soon after she got home, when she got a text from him.

Jen, I just wanted to tell u Im sorry about 2day. If u just want 2 b friends, I need to respect that. And besides, like u said, we r only 13! U could dump Elijah yet! Just kidding.

Relief coursed through her. She pondered her response for a few minutes. She wanted to compliment him on his maturity, but she didn't know how to do so without sounding like an adult complimenting a middle-schooler. Finally she answered him.

Miguel, thanks :-). U R so much more mature than most guys our age! And I do want to be your friend, so I am happy you are okay with that.

The next day, Wednesday, went better than the day before. Lucy was back in school. She still seemed under the weather, and participated little in the conversation at lunch, but Miguel didn't speak as freely with Lucy present. Also, in keeping with his text the previous day, he seemed to be making an extra effort to be nice to Jen and show her there were no hard feelings. Jen thought Lucy might have noticed and wondered why, but if so, she didn't comment.

Lucy was very quiet in art class. "Still not feeling well?" Jen asked her.

"Not really." Lucy looked away. It seemed to Jen more like a bad mood than illness; Lucy wasn't coughing or sneezing, though she did appear rather pale. Whichever it was though, illness or just a bad mood, Lucy resisted all attempts at conversation, so they worked in silence for most of the hour.

Later, after school, Lucy said she had something to do and wouldn't be taking the bus home. Jen asked her why, but Lucy wouldn't say.

"Just something I have to do," Lucy said.

Something told Jen that Lucy wouldn't have a sense of humor about it if Jen tried to hassle her, so she just said she'd see her the next day and got on the bus. She was sitting alone, staring out the window and watching the other kids board the bus, when Melanie's voice jerked her from her thoughts.

"Can I sit with you?" Melanie was standing by her seat.

"Sure, you can sit here," Jen said. "But don't you want to sit with your own friends?"

Melanie shrugged. "My friends will survive if I sit with you for a day," she said with a smile.

Jen smiled back. "Well, then, that would be great," she said.

Melanie slid into the seat beside her. "Where's that girl you usually sit with?"

"She said she had something to do and wouldn't be taking the bus."

"Maybe she had detention," Melanie said.

"What makes you say that?"

"She just seems like the type."

Jen had to concede the point, but said, "Well, I think she would have just told me that, though."

"Why are you friends with her anyway? She doesn't seem like your type of person. She's not that Katie chick you went to the mall with the other day, is she?"

"No, her name's Lucy. And how is it you even know anything about her? Have you ever even talked to her?"

"No, but my friend Sara, her sister's in eighth grade, and when we were at the mall just a couple of weeks ago we saw a group of eighth-graders. Sara's sister said it was the druggie crowd. Lucy was there. I didn't know her name, but I recognized her from the bus. I don't think mom and dad would be happy you're friends with her."

"She doesn't sit with the druggie crowd at lunch," Jen said.

"Really?" Melanie asked, her tone skeptical.

"No, she sits with Miguel and me."

"Well, maybe she's not as bad as some of those other kids," Melanie said uncertainly. "But I still doubt mom and dad would be happy about it."

"Maybe not, " Jen agreed. "But it's not like I'm going to do drugs with her or something."

"No, I know," Melanie said.

"I just think she could use a friend," Jen said. "Some people can maybe avoid falling in with the wrong crowd if they have a good friend."

"Maybe," Melanie said. "But Mom and Dad might be worried it would be the other way around—that she would pull you into the bad crowd."

"Well, she won't." Jen had known some parents who were worried about Lucy's influence on their kids last year. She found it ironic that now HER parents might be concerned. This universe appeared to have a warped sense of humor.

"You know, you seem—different these days," Melanie observed.

Oh geez. Jen swallowed hard and asked, "Different how?"

"Well, for the last few days, since that day you passed out, you've just seemed kind of different. I don't know. Almost like a grown-up. You never give me a hard time or tease me anymore. Was passing out like a near-death experience or something?"

Jen laughed. "I don't think I was *that* near death."

"Because I've heard about that," Melanie said as if Jen hadn't spoken. "People who have near-death experiences and then they have some sort of spiritual awakening. Did you see a bright light or anything?"

"Mel, I wasn't near death! I just passed out. I didn't see a bright light. And I don't know if not teasing you for a few days qualifies as a spiritual awakening."

"Well, even if you didn't." Melanie regarded her. "Something still seems different."

"Well, you know teenagers," Jen joked. "We're moody and changeable."

But Melanie still wouldn't let it drop. "How come you never talk about Morgan and Kenetia anymore?"

Stay cool, she told herself. Melanie could never figure out the truth. What could anyone in her family ever do if they thought she just didn't seem to be the same old Jen? Accuse her of hiding the real Jen somewhere? *If they think you're crazy, there's always the adolescent psych ward*, she reminded herself grimly. Acting a little different hardly qualified as crazy, though.

"Well, I've made some friends here now," she said to Melanie. "It's not like I've abandoned my old friends just because I don't text them every second anymore or talk about them constantly."

"But you were always texting Morgan and Kenetia and talking about them all the time and saying how much you missed them and all that. Now for the last few days you haven't done that at all." She studied Jen. "Are you depressed or something?"

The question reminded Jen of how she had often thought Melanie had missed her calling, that she should have been a therapist rather than a computer programmer. In fact, Mel's partner was a school counselor. Jen had sought out her advice about Lucy several times.

Melanie looked a little worried, so Jen smiled and said, "Don't worry." She patted Melanie's hand. "I'm not depressed. I'm fine. I'm just getting adjusted; that's all."

Melanie seemed unconvinced. "Are you sure? Because I saw this program on teen suicide the other night and—"

"Melanie! I'm sure," Jen said, laughing gently at Melanie's earnestness. "Why were you even watching that?"

"I was bored," Melanie said nonchalantly.

"And I'm sure this program provided tons of fun and excitement," Jen said.

"Well, okay, it wasn't really *fun*," Melanie conceded. "But it was interesting."

"Didn't it upset you?" Jen asked.

"Well, I felt bad that some kids would feel that upset," said Melanie. "I just can't understand why someone would do that."

Jen thought about the dark days after Josh had first left. She hadn't actively considered suicide, but sometimes she had just wished she wouldn't wake up in the morning. "It's a horrible thing," she said slowly, "but sometimes things just get so bad you can't ever imagine feeling good again."

Melanie glanced at her sharply. "You sound like you know."

"No, no," Jen said. "I've never been suicidal. But—" she supposed she shouldn't even say she'd known people who'd considered it. Melanie would ask tons of questions and maybe even tell their parents. Geez, this was the longest conversation

EVER. How long *was* this fucking bus ride, anyway? She glanced out the window and noted with relief that they'd almost reached their stop.

"But what?" Melanie persisted.

"But I've read books about depressed and suicidal people," Jen said finally, having no idea what else to say.

"Oh," Melanie said. "Okay." She seemed vaguely disappointed Jen hadn't had something more interesting to say.

Finally they were at their stop.

Chapter Nine

The next morning Lucy wasn't on the school bus again. Jen couldn't help but wonder why. Sure, Lucy might just be sick with some mild bug that wouldn't quite go away. She had looked rather pale the day before, and the grouchiness could have been related to not feeling well. But Jen couldn't shake the feeling something else was wrong.

The feeling was confirmed when Melanie caught up with her as they were getting off the bus at school. "Jen, Sara and her sister told me something bad about your friend Lucy."

"I'm not sure I want to hear it," Jen said.

"No, listen. They said Lucy's in the hospital."

"What? Why? She wasn't that sick. She only missed a day, and then yesterday I thought she might still be not feeling so great, but it didn't seem like anything serious—"

"Not that. She tried to commit suicide!"

Horror froze Jen into place. "Are you sure?"

"That's what Sara's sister says."

"Maybe it's just a rumor," Jen said. Sara's sister had already said Lucy was a druggie. Which, for all Jen knew, might be true, but maybe Sara's sister was just gossiping.

But Melanie was shaking her head. "I don't think so. Sara and her sister live just down the street from Lucy. They saw the ambulance and everything."

"Did they actually see it was Lucy who needed the ambulance?" Jen was grasping at straws, but maybe Lucy had been unable to wake her drunk, passed-out mother and had called the ambulance . . . also not good, but better than Lucy trying to commit suicide.

"Yeah. They went outside to see what was going on. Half the neighborhood was watching."

"How do they know she was trying to commit suicide though? Maybe there was some kind of accident," Jen said, which sent her mind to a bad place also, because she worried about domestic violence. Lucy's mother probably hadn't picked the best boyfriend . . .

"Sara and her sister were pretty close; they could hear some of what people were saying. Plus Lucy's mother was screaming—asking Lucy what she was thinking, and telling the paramedics Lucy had taken valium and alcohol."

"God, how awful!" Jen said. "Can you please try not to spread this around? It will be hard enough for Lucy as it is."

"I won't tell anyone else, but I don't think it'll matter. It's going to be all over school no matter what I do." Melanie was right, Jen realized.

A horrible thought occurred to Jen. "Did Brianna take any pictures or make a video with her phone?"

"No. Her parents took away her phone for a week for something she did; I don't know what."

"What about Sara?"

"No, she doesn't have a phone yet."

"Thank God." Jen sighed with relief. At least they wouldn't be posting anything to YouTube or Facebook.

"Poor Lucy," Jen said. "I know you're right, and the last thing she needs is people hassling her."

"I guess, but what can you do about it?" Melanie asked.

Jen thought for a second. "Not much, maybe, but I'll try to see a counselor before I go to class and tell her what happened."

"Good idea," said Melanie. "I don't think the school will be able to stop all the rumors though."

"Probably not, but the counselor can at least talk to some of her friends maybe and make sure they're okay."

"True. I'd be really upset if a friend of mine did that," Melanie said. As if remembering their conversation from the previous afternoon, Melanie peered intently at Jen. "How are you? You must be upset, too."

Jen smiled reassuringly at Melanie. "I'm okay. I promise."

"Are you sure? Because the program I watched said these kinds of things can be contagious. Like if a kid has a friend who commits suicide, she might try it, too."

"I'd never do that, I promise." But what an odd coincidence that Melanie had been discussing that very topic on the bus just yesterday and then Lucy had gone and done this just last evening. "Don't worry, okay?" Jen gave her a quick hug. "Now I have to hurry if I want to catch the counselor before class, okay?"

"Okay," said Melanie. They'd arrived at Melanie's locker, so Jen left her there, made a quick stop at her own, and then hurried to the eighth-grade counselor's office.

Carina Noble, the eighth-grade counselor, was wrapping up a conversation with another student when Jen arrived at her office. As the other student was leaving, Carina spied Jen in the doorway. "Jen, hey, how are you? Come on in."

Jen was momentarily startled. Carina sounded just like she had when Jen had come to consult with her in her previous life. But how did Carina know her in this one?

"M-Mrs. Noble," Jen stumbled a bit as she said her name, nearly forgetting as she often still did with the teachers and other staff that she couldn't just call her Carina. She walked into the office and sat down in a chair in front of Carina's desk.

"How is your mom? I know she was concerned when you first started here, about how you'd adjust and everything."

So that was how she knew Jen. Her mom had probably asked Carina to check in with Jen and make sure she was okay.

"My mom is fine." Jen didn't know how much she should say. She of course had no idea when she'd last talked to Carina in this life, except it hadn't been in the last several days for sure. "We like it here."

"Great!" Carina beamed. "So what brings you in here today?"

"Well, did you hear what happened to Lucy Morrison?"

"Lucy Morrison. . ." Carina was clearly trying to place the name.

This puzzled Jen. Last year, they'd worked together a lot in trying to help Lucy. Carina should have known who Lucy was without having to think about it.

But this was a different universe. And only some things were the same.

Carina was looking Lucy up on the computer. "Lucia Morrison—is this her?"

"Yes, but she goes by Lucy," said Jen. Lucy's father was white, but her mother was Hispanic. "I thought you might know her. She told me a teacher—Mrs. Jensen—spent a lot of time trying to help her last year. I thought maybe she talked to you too."

"Maybe—I guess Mrs. Jensen did come to me a few times last year about a student named Lucy," Carina was struggling to remember. The Mrs. Jensen in this universe must not have sought Carina out as much.

"So anyway, I guess you didn't hear," Jen went on. "But I heard Lucy tried to commit suicide last night."

"Oh my goodness!" Carina said. "Are you sure? You need to be careful not to spread rumors."

It sounded like a lecture, and it annoyed Jen. She wasn't sure she liked the Carina in this universe as much as the one in her old life.

"I'm not spreading rumors," she said. "I'm telling you." She tried to keep the edge out of her voice. "My sister is friends with her neighbors, and they said an ambulance came and everything." She proceeded to tell Carina the story Melanie had told her.

The conversation did get better. Carina did take her seriously once she explained everything. She asked some of the same questions Jen had asked Melanie, like how they knew for sure the ambulance was there for a suicide attempt, but Jen figured that was understandable. She promised to talk with Melanie's friend's eighth-grade sister right away and have the sixth-grade counselor talk to Sara to see how the sisters were feeling and to try to stop them from spreading the story around. Jen was hard-pressed to name other friends of Lucy's who might be upset by the news.

"She sits with our friend Miguel and me at lunch. Miguel is new here and I haven't been here that long either. I only have art class with Lucy, and I haven't really seen her hang out with anyone else."

Carina asked if Jen thought Miguel would be upset. Jen figured he'd be concerned, but she doubted he would be unduly traumatized as they weren't close and hadn't known each other long. Carina asked for his full name anyway, which Jen gave her. She said she would alert Lucy's teachers and have them send down any students who might be upset. By the time they finished talking, Jen was late to her first block, so Carina wrote her a pass. She felt better as she left, but she still thought the Carina in this universe lacked a certain—warmth—that she'd had in Jen's previous one. Or was that just how she came across to students? It troubled Jen that maybe Carina didn't come across to students as the warm, caring person the adults saw.

Maybe she's just having an off day, Jen thought. She hoped that's all it was. It was also strange to have people she'd known for years treat her like a different, much younger person. That in itself could be part of the reason for her uneasiness. She doubted she'd ever get used to that. Of course, if she stayed here long enough, she'd have to get used to it.

At least she believed Carina would take care of things, though. Maybe the other students didn't have the same reaction to her.

Later, in Amy's class, Jen was preoccupied. She and Miguel were in the same group for group activities, and after class ended he asked her if she was all right.

"You seem—I don't know—upset or something," he said.

"I am a little preoccupied," Jen admitted.

"Why? What's wrong?"

Jen glanced around at the other kids leaving class. "I can't talk here. I don't want anyone to overhear. I'll tell you at lunch, okay?"

"Okay," Miguel said.

She didn't know whether it was the right thing or not, but she figured she should tell him. He might hear it from someone else, and if Carina hadn't talked to him, she'd rather he heard it from her. Jen knew he wasn't the type to gossip, especially since he didn't know many kids here yet.

When their next block ended, Miguel approached her. "So what's up?" he asked.

Jen glanced around. "Let's wait until we get to the cafeteria."

"Must be some big secret," Miguel said.

"I don't know how much of a secret it actually is," said Jen. "But I don't want to be responsible for spreading it around."

"Oh, okay."

Once they had gotten their lunches and sat down at their usual table, Miguel asked, "Where's Lucy? Are you going to tell her too?"

So he hadn't heard.

"It's about Lucy," she said. "You haven't heard anything?"

"No. Should I have?"

"Well, I'm glad you didn't," Jen said. "Maybe the rumors haven't been spreading much then. Things might be worse after lunch though."

"What's going on? Is Lucy all right?"

"Well, I guess not," Jen admitted. "But before I tell you, you've got to promise to keep this to yourself. It'll be hard enough for Lucy when she comes back to school."

"Yes, I promise!" Miguel was practically shouting. "Just tell me already!"

"Shhh!" Jen cautioned. "Lower your voice." She was a little surprised that Miguel seemed to be kind of freaking out. He seemed to be a nice enough kid, but he hardly even knew Lucy. Maybe he just couldn't stand suspense in general.

"Are you going to tell me or what?" Miguel demanded in a loud whisper.

Jen leaned forward and said softly, "Lucy tried to kill herself last night."

"WHAT?"

"I told you, lower your voice." Not that anyone was paying attention to them anyway.

"What?" Miguel said again, this time in a whisper.

"There's no gentler way to say it. Lucy tried to commit suicide last night. Or at least, she took enough of her mom's valium and alcohol so an ambulance had to be called."

Miguel just sat there a moment, stunned. "Are you sure?" he finally asked.

Jen nodded. "My sister heard it from someone who lives near them and saw the ambulance come and take Lucy away and everything. I don't know for sure if they really know she was trying to commit suicide. Maybe she acted without thinking. Or maybe she was drinking with some friends and then took some of her mom's Valium to try to sleep and it was too much."

"But she would know at least not to take a whole bunch of pills, right? If she was just trying to sleep?"

"I'm not sure how many pills she took," she told him. "And she probably wasn't thinking straight if she'd been drinking. So it may not have been a deliberate attempt, but it's pretty scary anyway."

"Yeah." Miguel agreed. "I—I don't know Lucy well. But I've never known anyone who tried that. Even if she didn't really mean it. She must have been feeling awful."

"Yeah," Jen agreed. "That's why I made you promise to keep it to yourself. Other people might be spreading it around, but I wanted us to at least try to keep it as quiet as possible."

"She's not going to want to come back," he said.

"No. But she'll have to, and we can at least try to make it as easy on her as possible."

"Yeah. We should." Miguel agreed. Then he asked, "So is she in the hospital or at home or what?"

"I don't know." Jen pulled her cell phone out of her jacket pocket. "I'll text her and see if she answers."

"What are you going to say?" Miguel asked, looking alarmed. "I mean, you can't ask her if she tried to kill herself in a text."

"Of course not. I'll just ask her if she's at home and if I can see her after school."

"Oh, okay."

She texted Lucy, but wasn't surprised when Lucy didn't reply. She knew she wouldn't be able to check again for awhile after the lunch period ended without risking getting it confiscated until the end of the day. They went outside after they finished eating. Miguel had just joined the track team and a couple of his teammates tried to get him to shoot hoops, but Miguel shook his head and continued to talk to Jen.

"You don't have to worry about me, you know," she told him. "You can play with them."

"No, it's okay," Miguel said.

They leaned against the building and continued to talk. "Why do you think she did that?" Miguel asked.

"I don't know, but I do know her home life is pretty messed up," Jen said. "I—" she stopped herself when she realized she was going to reveal how she had tried to help Lucy when Lucy was her student last year.

"What?" Miguel asked.

"Well, just, you know, she has family issues, like a lot of kids do. Her parents got divorced last year, her mom has a new boyfriend, and it doesn't sound like he's so great. And I don't think her mom would win any parenting awards in any case."

"Yeah," Miguel said, "but I know lots of kids who have bad home lives." *And they don't do anything like this,* was the unspoken implication.

"I know. But her situation might be worse than most. She doesn't tell me everything. Or maybe she has a harder time handling it for some other reason; maybe she's prone to depression because of her brain chemistry or something."

"I have an aunt who's on antidepressants," said Miguel.

"Yeah, I know people on antidepressants too. Some people are just more likely to get depressed."

"You know, I heard—" Miguel looked around—"I heard she was a druggie. I don't want to spread rumors, but one of the guys on the track team said she hung with a druggie crowd. He saw us sitting together at lunch. He said he had never seen you with that crowd, but Lucy hung out with them sometimes and that's who she usually sat with at lunch until she started sitting with us." He looked down. "I don't want to say anything bad about your friend, but I thought you should know."

"It's all right. I heard that too. I didn't know at first because I haven't been here long. I got to know her because I ride the same bus and she has art class with me. And if she'd rather sit with us than the druggie crowd, that's probably better for her." She decided not to mention the fact that she was pretty sure Lucy wouldn't have bothered to sit with her if Miguel hadn't been there.

"What if people think *you're* a druggie because you're her friend?" Miguel asked. He didn't mention whether he worried for himself.

"I don't think they will if they don't see me hanging out with her other friends. Hopefully it will work the other way around and people will think Lucy has turned over a new leaf."

"Maybe you're right," said Miguel, but he sounded unsure.

Just then the bell rang. Jen checked her cell phone. Lucy hadn't texted her back.

"Anything?" Miguel asked.

"Nope," Jen said, putting her cell phone away.

During art class she couldn't help but obsess over Lucy. The fact that she normally spent that time with her made matters worse, especially since there wasn't anyone else at their table to talk to. Not only that, but she could hear people talking and she caught Lucy's name a couple of times. She couldn't hear what else they were saying. The room was quite noisy as everyone except her was talking while they worked, but she assumed that Lucy's story had made the rounds. She figured the reason she and Miguel hadn't heard any gossip before was that the kids in the hi-cap classes maybe didn't even know Lucy, but Jen was with a different group of kids in art class. She tried to just focus on her art project and not think about anything else, but it wasn't easy.

At the end of the day, for what seemed like the millionth time, she again checked her cell phone for messages. There were none. She considered. She didn't know exactly where Lucy lived, but she knew which bus stop was hers. She could get off at Lucy's stop and pay her a visit. Melanie's friend Sara and her sister got off at the same stop. They could tell her which house was Lucy's.

If only she could do this without telling Melanie.

A cover story was out. Melanie would see her getting off at Sara and her sister's stop and know something was up. No, she had to tell Melanie the truth.

As soon as she gathered the books she'd need from her locker, she went to go find Melanie and tell her what she wanted to do.

"I don't think that's a good idea," Melanie said right away.

"I just want to make sure she's okay. I won't stay long. Then I'll walk home. It's not far."

"But you've never been over there before. What if it's awful? Sara said Lucy's mom is crazy . . ."

Jen was getting tired of what Sara and her sister were saying. "Look, I don't even have to go inside if it looks like a bad situation. I'll be home before Mom and Dad are."

"Well, maybe you shouldn't go alone. I could come with you," Melanie suggested.

The suggestion surprised Jen. She hadn't thought Melanie would want to come anywhere near this mess. She was touched by her concern.

"Well—I'm sure I'll be fine, but you can come if you want," said Jen. Maybe she should be trying to shield her sister from whatever might await them, but she rather liked the thought of company.

"Cool!" Melanie now seemed excited about a prospect that a minute ago she thought was a bad idea. Jen figured being included made her feel important. She sat next to Jen on the bus again, peppering her with questions. What should they do in this situation or that one? Had she talked to Lucy? Had Lucy seemed depressed? What was she like as a friend?

Jen answered Melanie's questions as patiently as she could. Fortunately, the bus ride was much shorter when they got off at Lucy's stop. They followed Sara and her sister—whom Jen was dismayed to realize was her arch nemesis from PE, Brianna—and two other kids off the bus. She'd seen Brianna on the bus before, but hadn't realized that she was Sara's sister. *Great,* she thought.

"Mel, why are you getting off here?" Sara asked, glancing back at them as they stepped off the bus.

"Jen wants to check on Lucy," Melanie replied. "Can you tell us which house is hers?"

"Are you sure you *really* want to go over to that freak's house?" Brianna asked, her voice heavy with disdain.

"Brianna!" Sara said. "She's Jen's friend."

Brianna regarded Jen. "Maybe you should pick better friends."

"I'll keep it in mind, Brianna, but right now we just need to know which house is Lucy's," Jen said, struggling to keep her voice civil. Brianna was an uber-bitch, and she probably got away with it because she was your typical cool, blond, popular type.

"It's the yellow one on the corner," Sara said.

"Thanks," Jen said, hurrying away from them and pulling Melanie after her.

Lucy's house looked rather unkempt, with the yellow paint faded and peeling. The lawn needed to be mowed. The house stood out for these things in this neighborhood. Most of the houses and yards were well-kept, as well as being quite a bit larger.

There was no car in the driveway. Maybe it was in the garage, Jen thought. Surely even a mother with Lucy's mom's dubious parenting skills wouldn't have left her alone?

"Do you think she's home?" Melanie asked.

"I don't know," Jen replied. "I don't think her mother would have left her alone, but maybe her car is in the garage."

"Maybe," Melanie said. "Jen? Are you sure this is such a good idea?"

"Don't be silly," Jen said, with more confidence than she felt. "We're just dropping in on my friend from school." She tried her best to hide her uneasiness from Melanie. She wasn't quite sure why she felt so uneasy. She had met Lucy's mother last year. Though Lucy's mother hadn't impressed Jen as a competent parent, or a particularly competent adult, for that matter, she had been nice enough. She would probably think it was nice that Lucy's friends from school had come over to see her.

Of course, maybe Lucy's mother's drunk, angry boyfriend would greet them at the door.

Best not to think about that.

Would Lucy want to see them? Jen was not at all sure she would, but she wanted to at least try.

"Come on, it will be fine," she said, turning to smile at Melanie.

"If you say so," said Melanie, following her up the walk, "but I've heard the police have come here a couple of times because of loud arguments."

Somehow this didn't surprise Jen.

"Keep your voice down," Jen said, dropping her voice to a whisper. "If we can see her mom's boyfriend is there, we won't go in."

"Okay," Melanie whispered back.

They reached the small, unadorned front porch and climbed the steps. Jen rang the bell and heard it chime, but didn't hear any evidence of anyone moving through the house to answer the door.

"Let's go," Melanie said. "No one's home."

"Well, no one's had a chance to come to the door yet," Jen said. But as several moments passed and still no one came to the door, she had to concede that apparently no one was home.

"I guess I'll just try to call her later," she said as they turned to go.

As they walked home, Melanie had more questions. "Do you think she'll be all right?" she asked Jen.

"I hope so," Jen answered. "I just hope kids like Brianna leave her alone."

"Me too."

They walked in silence for a moment. Then Melanie asked, "When do you think she'll come back to school?"

"I don't know," said Jen. "I guess it just depends on how she's feeling—both physically and emotionally."

"Should we try to visit her again on Monday if she's not back yet?"

"Maybe. I might be able to talk to her over the weekend, and if I do, I'll ask her if she wants company."

Melanie nodded sagely. "Probably a good idea." She sounded so sober and adult that Jen wanted to burst out laughing, but she knew Melanie would get mad if she did.

Jen spent the rest of the afternoon and evening worrying about Lucy. An hour or so after they got home, she tried to call her, but Lucy didn't answer her cell and Jen ended up leaving a voice mail.

At dinner Jen's mother asked her a question that threw her for a loop.

"Jen, do you know a girl named Lucy Morrison?"

"What?" Jen almost choked on a mouthful of chicken.

"Lucy Morrison. She's an eighth-grader at your school. I don't think from the sound of it she'd be in hi-cap classes though, so you might not know her."

"She rides our bus," Melanie said. Jen glared at her. "Oops!" Melanie covered her mouth with her hand.

"So you guys do know her then?" her mother asked, looking from one daughter to the other.

There was no point in denying it. Jen just hoped Melanie wouldn't reveal anything more than Jen was willing to tell their mother. "Yes, I sit with her on the bus sometimes and she's in my art class. She's not a close friend or anything."

Melanie wisely, if a bit belatedly, kept silent.

Their mother looked concerned. "Have you heard anything about Lucy today, Jen?"

Melanie and Jen exchanged glances. Jen hesitated. "Yeah," she admitted. "I heard she tried to commit suicide last night." She glanced at Melanie with a warning look, but Melanie was just staring, her eyes as big as the proverbial dinner plates. She wouldn't have said it straight out if Ben had been there, but he and their dad were at some father-son thing for Ben's preschool, so it was just the three of them for dinner. Still, her mother glanced over at Melanie, warning Jen with her eyes not to say too much in front of her.

"It's okay, Mom," Jen said. "She already knows. Her friend lives down the street from Lucy and they saw the ambulance and everything. Melanie found out before I did. I went and spoke to a counselor this morning about it."

You went and spoke to a counselor? You must have been pretty upset then." Her mother's brow furrowed with concern.

"Of course I was upset. But I went to talk to the counselor because I was worried Melanie's friend and her sister might be spreading the word around about what happened. I thought maybe the counselor could talk to them or something. Things are going to be bad enough for Lucy without people saying nasty things behind her back."

"That was a very mature and kind thing for you to do," her mother said. "But I'm concerned about this Lucy. The receptionist at work has a daughter who also goes to your school. I guess they know Lucy and her parents pretty well, and they say she's really had problems since her parents divorced last year. They think she's into drugs and everything. I'm sorry she's having so much trouble, but I'm not sure she's a good friend for you to have."

"Mom, it's not like she's going to get me into drugs or something." Jen was having the oddest sense of deja vu. She could remember having similar conversations from time to time with her parents over one friend or another, but of course the last time had been maybe twenty years ago.

"I know, honey, but peer pressure can be tough to resist, and she just sounds like a very troubled young woman."

"Well, I think she is," Jen agreed. "But all I've done is sit with her on the bus and hang out with her a little bit at school. She hasn't tried to offer me drugs, nor has she seemed high at school or introduced me to any druggie friends."

"Well, just be careful," her mother said. "And I don't want you going over to her house."

"Of course not," Jen agreed, praying Melanie could keep it together and not spill the beans about going over there that afternoon, even though no one had answered the door. Melanie was a horrible liar, a trait Jen normally found endearing. She glanced over at Melanie, who seemed focused on keeping her lips clamped shut. It made Jen want to laugh, though she restrained herself.

"Okay then," said her mom, but she still looked worried.

"Don't worry, mom," Jen said. "It'll be okay. I think Lucy's just going through a tough time right now."

"That's right, and you girls know you can come and talk to me about anything, right? If you're feeling sad or upset, it's not good to bottle things up."

"We know, mom," Melanie said, apparently deciding it was safe to speak. "I don't think I'd ever be *that* upset about anything, but I think maybe her life isn't so great. I mean, her parents just got divorced and her dad lives far away, and I heard her mom's boyfriend is pretty gross and he and her mom drink all the time. And her house—ick. At least from the outside."

"We drive past her house on the bus," Jen said quickly, because she could tell their mom was wondering how Melanie knew that. "And Melanie, I think it's true Lucy's home life isn't so great, but you know it doesn't help when you gossip about the details like that."

"I'm not gossiping!" Melanie retorted. "I'm telling you guys, not spreading bad things about her at school or anything."

"I know. And it's one thing to discuss it here . . ."

"I know, I know. I won't spread it around at school," Melanie said, her tone one of exaggerated weariness. "But it's not like people aren't already talking about it as it is."

"I know. We just don't want to add to the gossip."

"I'm glad to hear you girls know better than to spread this around at school," their mother said. "Things will be hard enough for her as it is, but I do want you to promise me you won't go over to her house. From what I've heard, I think Melanie is right about her home life not being so great. And that's not her fault, but I don't want you over there, with what I've heard about drugs and unsupervised parties and all that."

Jen avoided looking at Melanie. "Okay, Mom."

She wondered whether she would be able to keep that promise or not.

Chapter Ten

Jen awoke the next morning thinking of Lucy. She reached for her phone on the nightstand and checked for messages. Nothing. *Damn*!

She sent Lucy another text, saying she was worried about her and to please contact her as soon as possible, then went to take a shower. While she dressed and ate breakfast, she kept her phone beside her, but Lucy never replied.

After breakfast, she tried to do her homework, but she couldn't concentrate. Before long, she decided to break her promise to her mother and go over to Lucy's house.

She needed a cover story, so she asked her mother if she could take the bus to meet her friend "Katie" at the mall.

"Sure, but I could drive you if you want."

"No, that's okay. I like riding the bus."

"You sure are getting independent," her mother observed. "You never used to like taking the bus."

Jen said, "Well, in eighth grade, it's cooler."

Her mother smiled. "I should have known," she said. "Kids in middle school like to pretend they don't have parents."

Jen considered walking to Lucy's, but decided to save time by taking the bus. When she got off a block away from Lucy's, though, she sort of wished she had walked instead. The bus ride was entirely too quick and she still wasn't sure what she'd say to Lucy.

So it was with some trepidation Jen headed up the front walk to Lucy's house. She hoped Lucy answered the door herself and not a hostile parent or parent's boyfriend.

She knocked. No response. She knocked again. She was ready to leave when the door opened.

Lucy's mother was barely past thirty; at least she had been in Jen's other life. She'd told Jen she gave birth to Lucy at age seventeen. Despite a hard life which included heavy drinking, smoking, and, Jen suspected, domestic violence, Jen's mother looked very young as she stood there in the doorway. She might have passed for twenty-five. The resemblance between Lucy and her was obvious. They both had thick black hair, though Lucy wore hers shoulder-length and her mother's was waist-length. Normally a shade darker than Lucy's, her skin appeared unusually pale today, except for the dark circles under her eyes. She wore a bathrobe, though it was mid-day. Jen assumed she'd been up late worrying about Lucy. Despite her significant shortcomings as a parent, Jen did believe she genuinely loved Lucy.

"Mrs. Morrison?" she asked timidly. When Lucy's mother didn't respond right away, she said, "I'm a friend of Lucy's. I just wanted to check on her. I'm worried about her."

It seemed to take Mrs. Morrison a long time to process the information. Finally she said, "You're Lucy's friend?"

"Yes. We ride the school bus together and she's in my art class. Can I see her?"

"You're Lucy's friend? Have I met you before?" Lucy's mother didn't sound hostile, but rather befuddled, as though she were having trouble making sense of the conversation.

"No, I've never been here. Did I wake you or something? I'm sorry if I'm bothering you." Jen was starting to wonder if Lucy's mother had refilled the prescription for sleeping pills and then taken one or two too many herself. She hoped if she had refilled it, she had at least had the sense to keep the pills locked away. But maybe Mrs. Morrison was acting so befuddled because she had hardly slept.

"No, it's all right." Mrs. Morrison stepped aside and opened the door wider so Jen could come in. "It's nice of you to visit. And you can call me Cristina."

"Thanks. I'm Jennifer Edwards, but everyone calls me Jen."

"I guess you heard what happened," Cristina said, looking terribly sad.

"Yeah. I mean, is it true?" Jen asked awkwardly. "Did she really. . . I mean, I don't mean to invade her privacy, or yours—"

"Have a seat, please." Cristina indicated a sagging, mud-brown couch. Jen sat down cautiously. She thought it smelled faintly of alcohol, but maybe she was imagining things. Cristina sat in an overstuffed recliner across from her that was a different shade of brown than the couch and began telling Jen what had happened.

"She took some of my sleeping pills and chased them with alcohol. I know all the stories about wild parties here, but I didn't even know she had been helping herself to our beer and wine coolers. I guess—" she paused, looked down. "Manny and I were drinking so much ourselves we didn't notice that more was missing. I thought this was the first time Lucy had done it, but after they pumped Lucy's stomach, she told me she did it all the time. I guess—well, I guess I have a problem." She broke off and looked down again. "So I'm going into rehab. I'm leaving for an inpatient unit in a few days here. I guess I'm not a good mother if Lucy did this."

Jen gaped at her. She couldn't believe Cristina had admitted all this to her, a virtual stranger, and, to all appearances, a thirteen-year-old. Had the woman's boundaries always been this poorly defined? Maybe so. She had just admitted she needed an inpatient unit for her alcoholism. This had to be an emotional low point for her, given what Lucy had done. At least Cristina was trying to take responsibility, though. Jen gave her credit for that.

"I'm glad you're getting help," Jen said. "But what's going to happen to Lucy while you're in rehab?" A horrible thought occurred to her. "She's not staying with—Manny—is she?" She doubted Cristina's boyfriend was parent material.

The expression that crossed Cristina's face told Jen Cristina agreed with her. "Dear lord, no. Manny's gone. I kicked him out.

No, Lucy's going to stay with my sister in Seattle. She'll have to change schools, of course, but she can go to private school there and my sister knows a good therapist. It's close to my rehab clinic, so she'll be able to see me when I'm allowed visitors. If she wants." The corners of Cristina's mouth sagged downward. "I don't know if she'll want to."

"Well . . ." Jen fumbled over what to say. "I think you're doing the right thing, getting help."

"Sure, and Lucy only had to try to kill herself first!" Cristina said bitterly.

"But she didn't succeed, thank God, so it's not too late."

"You seem like you're real smart." Cristina regarded Jen. "Mature. Not like Lucy's other friends. Are you in her grade?"

Jen had already mentioned having a class with her, but wasn't surprised Cristina hadn't processed that.

"Yes, we have art class together, and we ride the bus together."

"Well, I wish she had more friends like you."

"Thanks," said Jen. "Can I see her?" She hadn't heard anything at all from anywhere else in the house. She wondered if Lucy had been eavesdropping on their conversation.

"I'll ask her." Cristina looked uncertain. "I'm not sure if she'll want to, but I think it would be good for her."

"If she doesn't want to, I'll understand," said Jen.

Jen waited in the living room while Cristina disappeared down the hall. She heard her knock on Lucy's door and a muffled response. Cristina went into Lucy's room for a moment. Jen could hear them talking through the hollow door of Lucy's room, but not what they were saying.

Moments passed. Jen took the opportunity to look around the small living room. The rug, which needed a good vacuuming, was a flat, industrial blue-gray. The recliner in which Cristina had sat and the couch were the only places to sit. A brown wicker trunk that looked like a cat had clawed at it served as a coffee table. The blinds were drawn over the two windows in the room, making it dark and depressing. There were no curtains. No art or photographs adorned the ivory walls. The one extravagance was the large, flat-screen TV which dominated one wall. Jen figured that was Manny's or at least Manny's idea. Prison cells were probably more cheerful, though Jen supposed no one noticed when they watched the gigantic TV.

After what seemed an eternity, Cristina left Lucy's room and returned to the living room. "You can go on in. It's the last door on the right."

"Thanks," said Jen. She got up and headed to Lucy's room with some trepidation. She was glad Lucy had agreed to see her, but Cristina had been in her room so long Jen figured she must have had to do some convincing.

The short hallway branched off to the left from the living room. She passed the bathroom and a room on the left that was probably Lucy's mother's room. She knocked on Lucy's door. There was a moment of silence, long enough for her to think Lucy might not let her in after all, but finally Lucy said, "Come in."

Lucy was lying down on her unmade bed in sweats and a T-shirt. The only light in the room came from the open doorway and peeked in around the drawn shades.

"Hi, Lucy," Jen said softly.

"Hey," Lucy said flatly, staring up at the ceiling.

"Can I turn on the light?" Jen asked. "It's pretty dark in here."

Lucy switched on a small lamp next to her bed, giving the room an eerie glow. As with the rest of the house, the furniture was sparse—twin bed, bedside table, desk—but posters covered the walls. Most depicted bands Jen didn't recognize, but Lucy also had a big poster of the space needle. On top of the desk sat Lucy's laptop and cell phone.

Lucy sat up and faced Jen, but made no other effort to make her feel welcome. Jen pulled the chair from Lucy's desk over beside Lucy's bed, but once she sat down, she had no idea what to say.

"Your mom seems pretty worried about you," she finally said.

"Yeah, she's sorry now, right? Too bad I only had to try to kill myself to get her attention," Lucy retorted.

"Is that why you did it? To get your mom's attention?"

Jen thought Lucy might react angrily, but Lucy seemed to be considering the question. "Sort of, I guess," she answered. "But also I needed to get away from my stepfather, and I couldn't think of any other way."

A chill ran down Jen's spine. "Why did you need to get away from your stepfather?"

Lucy looked away. She hesitated so long Jen thought she might not answer. Finally she said, "He was . . . doing things to me."

"Oh my God," Jen said. "You mean . . ."

"I mean, he'd come into my bedroom when mom was at work and do things to me," Lucy said. "He's a fucking child molester."

"Lucy, how awful." Jen wanted to reach out and hug her friend, but something told her Lucy would not be comfortable with that. "Does your mom know? Is that why she kicked him out?"

"Yeah. He kept telling me she'd never believe me. I was afraid he might be right and didn't even try to tell her at first. But lately I've been trying to tell her. She wouldn't listen. She kept blowing me off, saying she had to get to work or do whatever. Then . . . " Lucy broke off.

"Then what?" Jen prompted after a long pause.

Finally Lucy continued, "When he came into my room that night, I was ready for him. Mom was at work, and he'd been drinking, the way he does sometimes after they've had a fight. That's when he's most likely to come into my room. They fight, he starts drinking, and she goes to work."

Jen nodded.

Lucy took a deep breath and continued. "He'd finished a bottle of Jack Daniels early in the evening and was in the living room snoring in the recliner. I knew he'd probably wake up in a few hours like he always does, and I took the empty bottle with me into the bedroom. I'd never even thought about fighting back before, but for some reason, seeing that empty bottle beside his chair, I did then. So I took the bottle, got ready for bed, got into bed and hid the bottle under the covers, turned off the light, and waited." Here she stopped again.

Jen waited.

Lucy continued. "He took so long I was starting to think he might not show up, but he did. I pretended to be asleep until he sat down on the bed and whispered my name. Then I brought my hand with the bottle in it up and hit him on the head as hard as I could. It broke the bottle."

"Oh wow! He deserved it! Then what happened?"

"He just looked stunned for a second. Then he fell off the bed and onto the floor. For a minute I wondered if I'd killed him. I got out of bed. I was going to get my cell phone off my desk and call 911, but he was in the way and he started moving, and I was afraid to stay in the room any longer, so I ran out and into the kitchen to use our landline. But I couldn't find the handset. I was running around looking for it and finally found it in the living room under a couch cushion.

"But he was right behind me! He grabbed me and spun me around. He shook me and said he'd kill my mother and then he'd take me away and he could do whatever he wanted.

"My mother came in just then. She came home early from work because it was slow there; she's a bartender at McNeary's Bar. She'd heard him!

"At first we just stood there. We hadn't heard her come in and didn't know she was there until she shouted my name. She was pissed! She may choose the wrong guys, but she's not easily intimidated, and hearing what he said made her mad, not scared.

"Manny suddenly was all 'oh, I'm so sorry, honey, you know I didn't mean it; Lucy just gets me so mad sometimes and I say things I don't mean'. I yelled that's not true, he's a total perv, ask him what he meant when he said he could 'do whatever he wanted'. Manny said I was lying, he would never do that, why would he want a child when he had her. Mom wasn't looking so mad and was starting to look confused, like she didn't know her head from her ass anymore. Manny told her to sit down and he'd fix her a drink and straighten everything out.

"Well, if she started drinking, she'd never listen to me. He'd get her to keep drinking until she passed out, and the next day, if she even remembered anything, he might be able to convince her it never happened. I ran into the kitchen and opened the cupboard where she keeps her sleeping pills. I found them and dumped all the pills in the bottle into my hand. Mom and Manny had followed me and mom was yelling, 'Lucy, what are you doing?' I shoved them all into my mouth before she could stop me. Then I pushed her aside and opened the fridge looking for something to wash down the pills. Some of her hard lemonade was in there—she loves that stuff—and I remember thinking she wouldn't have the pills or the hard lemonade. The pills were already starting to dissolve in my mouth and they tasted like shit. She tried to get the bottle from me, but I shoved her hard enough so she fell. I took a swig of lemonade and swallowed some of the pills.

"But now Manny was coming toward me and he was so pissed! I grabbed an unopened bottle of the lemonade from the fridge and hit him on the nose and blood started gushing from it. I couldn't believe the bottle didn't break. I drank more, trying to get more pills down. And that's when I passed out. I didn't think it would hit me so quickly. Maybe I was hyperventilating too or something. I woke up in the hospital."

"Oh my God," Jen said. She had been silent for several minutes while Lucy had been recounting her story, and she had no idea what to say now. "I'm so glad you're all right. And your mom, too. Did he try to hurt her too?"

"No. After I pushed her she got right back up and called 911. I guess we scared the shit out of her. Imagine that." Lucy laughed humorlessly.

"Anyway, mom tried to revive me and yelled at Manny, saying if I died it would be all his fault. He ended up storming off in his car right before the ambulance pulled up."

"She told me she kicked him out," Jen said.

"Well, that's not precisely true, but close enough I guess," Lucy said. "He hasn't been back. There's a warrant out for his arrest."

"Oh."

"Yeah."

"Well, that's good though, right?" Jen asked.

Lucy shrugged. "Yeah, I guess. At least he can't come back here. And mom can't allow him to come back anyway. This caseworker from Child Protective Services came and talked to me without mom and everything. Scared the shit out of me. I was afraid they'd put me in a foster home or something. But I'm sure she told them she had no idea what Manny was doing, which was true, and they must have believed her. I told them that too. Mom's got her flaws, but a foster home would be worse, I bet. But I bet she's worried now, since she's all of a sudden going into rehab and everything."

"She told me you were going to go stay with your aunt."

"Yeah," Lucy sighed. "It'll be okay, I guess. I don't know her very well, but I'd rather be in Seattle than here. Manny won't know where to look for us if he does decide to come back before the police get him. And Seattle's way cooler than here. Plus I bet everyone in school knows what I did." She regarded Jen, trying to determine if Jen had betrayed her or not.

"I didn't tell anyone," Jen said. "But still, people who live on your street saw the ambulance and all . . ."

"Yeah, like that bitch Brianna," Lucy said bitterly.

"Yeah. I didn't hear a lot of people talking about you or anything, but still. It would probably be hard to come back." Jen didn't think she should admit she had gone to see the counselor about her. While Lucy might appreciate her attempts to stop the gossip from spreading, Jen did not think Lucy would like the way she'd gone about it. So she just said, "It's better to start fresh."

"It's a private school, though," Lucy complained. "Everyone there is probably like Brianna."

"Maybe not," Jen said. "What's the name of the school? We should look it up online. Get an idea of what it's like."

"I guess we could." Lucy didn't sound enthusiastic, but she got up from the bed and got her laptop. She and Jen sat down on the bed with it and got online.

"Oh, my God, it's a creative arts school!" she moaned.

"It sounds interesting," Jen said. "What's the problem?"

"I'm not creative!"

Jen stared at her in surprise. "Yes, you are," she said. "You're really good in art. You'll probably like this school if you give it a chance." She leaned over the laptop and clicked through different pages of the website. "It doesn't sound like a place where a bunch of rich snobs go to school," she said. "There are lots of scholarships, so it's not like everyone there is rolling in money."

"Look at the kids, though. They look like a bunch of hippies!"

Jen regarded the pictures of the students. Their appearance didn't seem all that different than hers and Lucy's. "They do not. You've just made up your mind you're not going to like it. Give it a chance, at least."

Lucy didn't speak for a long moment. Finally she said, "Yeah, I guess anything's better than living here with Manny."

"Yeah, definitely. Hey—I don't mean to be rude, but how is your mom paying for private school, even one with lots of financial aid options?"

"She isn't. My aunt is rich, and she has connections at that school. She's paying for the rest of this year, but she thinks I can get a partial scholarship for next year."

"So you're staying there?"

Lucy shrugged. "It kind of sounds like it. So I guess I better hope the school doesn't suck too much. And I suppose I better pack. We're leaving on Monday."

"So soon?" Jen asked. "Then I might never see you again."

Lucy shrugged. "I'll text. But yeah, mom didn't want me to miss too much school, and she wanted to get started with her rehab and they had an opening."

Jen doubted Lucy would want a hug or a long, gushy good-bye, so she just said, "Well, I'll miss you."

"Well—hey. I'll keep in touch. I mean, your boyfriend lives in Seattle and you didn't break up with him. So there's no reason we can't still be friends, right?"

"Right," Jen agreed. She hoped Lucy didn't ask where Elijah lived, but if she did, Jen planned on naming an area far away from the school Lucy would be attending, so Lucy would figure it unlikely they would run into each other. "I hope you like your new school, Lucy. Is there anything you want me to tell people at our school, if they ask, about why you went away?"

"I guess it doesn't matter anymore," Lucy said. "Tell them whatever you want. I guess you can tell them I went to live with rich relatives and am attending some snobby private school."

"Okay." Jen smiled. She was startled when Lucy smiled back. The talking seemed to have improved Lucy's mood. She seemed happier and more energetic than when Jen had arrived.

Catching a glimpse of the time on Lucy's computer, she said, "Oh, I've been here almost two hours! I guess I better go. I want to catch the next bus. Promise me you'll call or text, okay?"

"I will. Take it easy."

As she was leaving, Cristina said, "Thanks for coming. How did she seem? She'll hardly even talk to me."

Jen felt sorry for Cristina, even though she'd been a lousy mother. She hoped she was successful in turning things around. "I think she'll be okay," she said. "She seems better now than when I got here. But don't try to push her to talk. Just give her space." She knew she shouldn't tell an adult what to do, but Cristina didn't seem to mind. Indeed, she was hanging on Jen's every word. "We looked up her new school on the web and everything."

"Oh, good. She hasn't been very excited about it. Or anything, for that matter. Well. Not that I blame her," Cristina said, chewing on her lower lip.

"Yeah," agreed Jen. "I think she's still not that enthusiastic, but I do think it's better than her going back to school here. At least there, she can get a fresh start."

"Exactly," Cristina agreed. "We both need that."

Chapter Eleven

Taryn spent several days mulling over Jen's story. She wanted to talk to the professor about it, but she hesitated. Should she admit to him what she suspected? She might get more information that way, unless he flipped out when she confronted him and clammed up.

Finally, about a week after she'd met Jen, Taryn made up her mind.

She got up bright and early, even though her first class wasn't until eleven. Dr. Murphy was always in his office by eight.

Taryn knocked once on his office door, but opened it without waiting for him to answer.

"Taryn!" Startled, Dr. Murphy looked up from his desk.

She didn't bother with hello, just took a deep breath and plunged ahead—"Dr. Murphy— I *have* to ask you something." He looked at her quizzically."What do you know about Jen Edwards's situation? The girl who came to see you a few days ago?"

The professor looked puzzled. "What are you talking about?" he asked, but his tone suggested he knew what she was talking about.

"I think you know." She tried to stare him down, met his eyes levelly, though as casually as possible. It actually seemed to be working—the professor broke eye contact first.

"No, I don't," he said, shaking his head.

"No?" she chided. "And I suppose you haven't been doing any secret experiments, either" Taryn said.

"You are WAY outside of your purview here, my dear. All you need concern yourself with are your studies, and *basic* research." Suddenly she felt like a kindergartener. "Besides," he snorted, "What would you presume to know about it?" She regarded him. Were his eyes actually twinkling? He was *so* arrogant. "Those aren't your concern. Besides, you have no idea what they're about."

"You'd be surprised," she said.

"Is that so?" the professor retorted. He seemed amused now. "And what do you *think* you know?" The professor's patronizing tone rankled. Dr. Murphy wasn't usually like this with her. It made her all the more convinced her suspicions were correct.

"I know they're related to time travel," she said.

"Is that what you think?" he said, noncommittally, though he appeared slightly rattled by this. Clearly it had never occurred to him that Taryn would suspect anything. "Well, even if that were true, what does it have to do with Ms. Edwards's situation?"

"Dr. Murphy, we've talked *dozens* of times about how time travel and parallel universes are related!" Taryn was losing patience. Did he think she wasn't paying attention when they'd had all those inspiring, heady conversations on these profound subjects? And here he was, being deliberately obtuse, insulting her intelligence. It stung. "You even explained the connection to Jen! She told me you did."

"You discussed this with her? What did you two talk about?" the professor demanded, his eyes narrowing.

"Nothing!" Taryn cried. He was starting to make her nervous. "Everything!" she corrected.

"You must tell me exactly what was said." Dr. Murphy regarded her with a steely gaze Taryn had never seen before.

"Okay," she said. He seemed to relax a bit, but Taryn wasn't willing to let this opportunity pass, despite the new, unsettling side of him she'd just seen. "But *only* if you tell me what you're working on," she said. "I won't tell anyone," she assured him. "Jen hasn't even said she wants to go back to her original universe."

"She might, though. Can you imagine what it must be like to have your entire existence wiped out and be thirteen again?"

Taryn shuddered. Still . . . "On the other hand, she gets the chance to start over, to apply her adult wisdom and make better choices in her life."

"Wouldn't we all like that," the professor agreed. "Still, her entire previous existence has been wiped out. She can't share memories of her past life with anyone, or have the same friends. Even her experiences with her family are different. This could lead to an existential crisis of monumental proportions."

"Gosh, I suppose so," Taryn agreed. But then she realized what the professor was implying."Are you saying you can travel in time, or between universes? Really? Have you done it? Oh my God, can I try it?"

"Don t even think about it!" the professor's voice was low but severe. "There is no way I'm involving you in this!"

"But why not?"

"Don't be absurd!" the professor snapped. "First, there's some physical risk involved. And of course interfering with events in the past could irrevocably alter future events, as anyone who saw *Back to the Future* could tell you."

"But wouldn't the alternate future just be in another universe? Couldn't you travel to a universe that's not messed up?"

"Traveling to another universe isn't as simple as booking a flight to Vegas. You can't always go exactly where you want to go. So if Jen wanted to go back to her original universe, I could try to send her back, but I might end up sending her somewhere else. The universe might just be slightly different than her old one, perhaps close enough so she would be happy with it. But it may be very different.

"That's why I've kept my research utterly secret. If anyone knew, people would want to try time travel or even go to a parallel universe where they'd hope their lives might be better. I don't want people pestering me, and I'm certainly not about to start helping people entertain themselves in such a way."

They were both silent a moment as Taryn digested this.

Finally she asked, "How do you think Jen got here in the first place?"

The professor chuckled ruefully. "I wish I knew. It doesn't make any sense to me that she got here involuntarily, accidentally, as it were."

Taryn was disappointed to hear that the professor, with all his knowledge and secret experimentation, couldn't explain that either. "So you really have no idea?"

"Well, no. I mean, it's as though she went through a wormhole by accident, but I don't see how she could have."

"Does your research involve wormholes? It's about the only thing I can think of for time travel to actually work. Isn't there *anything* you've found that might explain what happened to Jen?"

The professor's expression became more guarded. "One generally doesn't stumble into wormholes by accident," he said.

Taryn hesitated. She was afraid if she said the wrong thing, the professor would shut down. She wished she had taken more psychology classes. Finally she said, "Didn't Jen say anything about that day that might help explain things? Did you ask her about the exact events leading up to her coming here? All she told me was she was hit by a car."

"She told me the same thing. I was stunned by her account, too stunned to think of what else to ask her," the professor admitted. "It's not every day that a visitor from a parallel universe walks through the door!"

"I'll bet we could get more details if we asked her to come in again," Taryn said. "She wants to understand what happened.

We could maybe help her, and learn more about time travel and inter-universe travel." Taryn was warming to the idea. "Think about it. She came to you for help. You don't have to tell her about any experiments you're doing. You could just tell her you're trying to figure out what's going on."

The professor considered this. "That's not a bad idea."

"Dr. Murphy? Can I help? I so want to be a part of this." Taryn hated herself for the tentative note in her voice.

The professor thought for a long moment. Finally he said, "Do you know how to reach this girl?"

Hope lifted her heart. "Yes. She gave me her cell number."

"Okay. You call her and ask her to come back at her earliest convenience. And you can sit here with me while I talk to her and take notes. But do NOT tell her about any secret experiments. Do I have your word on that?"

"Of course," Taryn said. "I won't tell her anything."

"Good. Try to have her come in within the next few days."

Taryn knew not to ask anything else at this point; she didn't want to say anything to make Dr. Murphy change his mind about allowing her be there when he interviewed Jen. She knew when she was ahead. She whistled as she made her way to the parking lot.

Chapter Twelve

"It was an ordinary day," Jen told the professor and Taryn. "Right up until the time I got hit by the car."

Jen had been eager enough to see them again. Taryn had said she and Dr. Murphy wanted to learn more details of Jen's story, hoping to figure out what had caused her involuntary journey.

As near as Jen could tell, though, they were getting nowhere. She tried her best to answer their questions.

"Okay, you walked out into the street and got hit," Taryn said. "Do you remember what you saw right before and right after you got hit?"

"Right before I got hit all I remember seeing is Arabella's— my principal's—face. She was the one who hit me. Not on purpose, obviously. I had stepped out into the street without looking. I saw her behind the wheel and heard screeching brakes."

"And after you got hit?" the professor asked.

"Just floating in blackness for a long time. Then I awoke as a thirteen-year-old."

"Just blackness? Could you see anything at all? Or hear anything?"

Jen shook her head. "There were a couple of things I found out later, things that happened in this universe, but they probably aren't important."

The professor perked up. "Well, it's hard to be certain what's important and what isn't, so can you describe those events for me?" he asked.

"Okay. Well, like I said, probably not critical, but I wasn't the only one who wanted a fresh start. The other Jen wanted one as well."

"The other Jen? You mean the one who was really thirteen?"

"Yes."

The professor's brow furrowed. "And how do you know that?"

"By reading her journal. She kept one on her computer."

Jen had now read all of the other Jen's journal. Her adolescent self seemed well-adjusted until the Evan Steed incident. After that, her friends Morgan and Kenetia stuck by her, but others at school found out and she became a bullying target. Never mind that she hadn't done anything except be too trusting. Some of the kids had delighted in calling her a slut to her face and plastering it all over her Facebook wall. She'd actually been relieved when she and her family moved away from Seattle, though she missed Morgan and Kenetia.

The move was a chance for a fresh start, but things hadn't worked out so well. Though not a target of the kind of bullying she'd experienced in Seattle, she mentioned a "mean girl" (Brianna, maybe) who'd been giving her a hard time, and just a general difficulty making new friends. And the family had some money problems because her father had been jobless for a while before they moved. Plus, she'd been having nightmares about Evan since the day she met him, and they'd continued unabated. The adult Jen figured she hadn't told her mother, since her mother hadn't mentioned nightmares. The last entries of her journal were detailed fantasies about being an adult living in an exotic location with the perfect guy, though she admitted, after her experience with Evan, "I'm sort of afraid of guys now."

The professor's voice pulled her out of her thoughts. "It's interesting that you both had the same thought at approximately the same time, though it might not be meaningful. Lots of people have that wish at one time or another."

"True," Jen agreed. "But there is one other thing. I had a near-death experience, being hit by a car. And I'm wondering if maybe the other Jen was nearly killed as well. Apparently she'd spilled a glass of water onto a power strip in the middle of the night. Maybe she got up to use the bathroom, or she couldn't sleep and tried to turn on the bedside lamp to read. She may have gotten a shock and almost died. I don't know, of course. The lamp has never worked since I got here, though. Mom noticed the water glass and the damp spot around the power strip by Jen's bed. She gave me another power strip. She asked if I'd been shocked, but of course *I* hadn't."

The professor stared at her for a long moment. Jen began to feel rather stupid for saying anything. What was he supposed to do with this information, anyway?

Finally he spoke. "Well, obviously, no one knows what happens after death. No one who can let us know, at any rate. Hugh Everett was an atheist, but even so, he believed the Many Worlds Interpretation implied that humans are immortal. His daughter, a distinguished quantum physicist herself, committed suicide in 1997, and she left a note saying that after death she would be reunited with her father in a parallel universe. So some theorists do think we might travel to a parallel universe when we die. Most scientists, however, believe such matters are beyond the purview of science, which of course precludes them from even *talking* about such things."

"So . . . you mean . . . we switched places instead of dying? Or does being here mean I *am* dead, and instead of going someplace where all my dead relatives are waiting, I came here by accident?"

"I don't know." The professor frowned.

"So I might really be dead in my original universe." The thought filled her with sadness. She imagined Amy and her family, crying as her casket was lowered into the ground. She should have written a will, designating Melanie or Amy as Aquarius's caretaker. As it stood now, Josh would probably take her.

"Maybe," Dr. Murphy said. "But maybe not. And there's undoubtedly a similar universe where you are still alive."

The thought cheered Jen somewhat.

The professor then surprised her by changing the subject. "Tell me about your parents."

"What—what about them?" Why was he asking about her parents? Taryn seemed puzzled as well.

"Just tell me about their background. For example, where did they grow up?"

Jen answered some questions about her parents in both universes, growing more puzzled by the minute, until at last she said, "Professor, I don't mean any disrespect, but how is this helping you figure out what happened?"

The professor hesitated a moment before answering. "Just trying to get a good picture of you and your situation."

"Dr. Murphy, Jen's not a government spy or a terrorist or something, and neither are her parents."

Dr. Murphy peered intently over the top of his bifocals at Taryn. "*Do you mind?*" he said, his tone harsh. Both Taryn and Jen shrank back.

Anxious to mollify him, Jen said in a small voice, "I don't mind answering your questions. I was just wondering about them."

"I'm sorry," he said, "but you have to understand— I've been investigating, pondering these issues longer than the two of you have been alive." He looked very serious. "I've had plenty of time to think about the implications." He paused, collecting his thoughts. "This is my life's work. All along people have shown *great* interest. You have no idea how hard it's been to keep it in the realm of the purely theoretical." He shook his head ruefully. "I had to disclose just enough detail to keep my funding, but not give away the farm, as they say. No one suspects that I withheld some of the key pieces of the puzzle, the ones you need to put the theory into practice—and I plan to keep it that way! We must proceed with the *utmost* caution. I don't want information to fall into the hands of the wrong people."

"You mean like terrorists?" Jen asked. She supposed it made sense. Knowing how to travel forward or backward in time would be useful if you wanted to plant a bomb, or foil a terrorist plot.

"Yes, perhaps terrorists. Or the government. Or even people wanting me to help them travel through time or to another universe recreationally."

"But you haven't really told me anything anyway," Jen pointed out. Then she processed what the professor seemed to be implying. "Are you saying...*you can actually do these things? Is that* what you mean?"

The professor paled as he realized he had said too much.

Taryn jumped on it. "Maybe you should just tell us, Professor. We won't tell anyone. Who would believe us anyway?"

The professor hesitated for a long moment. Jen was beginning to wonder if he'd answer them at all. She glanced over at Taryn. Taryn, her expression grave, did not turn her gaze away from the professor.

Finally he said, "I must have your word—both of you—that you will keep everything I reveal to you an absolute secret. Probably no one would believe you anyway, but I don't want anyone poking around my lab."

"Of course I won't say anything," Taryn assured him.

"I won't say anything either, Professor," Jen echoed.

"But wait a minute—" Taryn exclaimed, "people poke around in your lab all the time. Geez, the administration even gives tours."

"Not *THIS* lab. Do you really think I would conduct such experiments in my campus lab?"

"I guess not," Taryn said. "Where is this secret lab, if you don't mind my asking?"

"I don t want to say anything else just now," Dr. Murphy said. "Tonight. Seven o'clock. Taryn, I'll give you directions to my house. Will that work for you, Jen?"

"Taryn, can you give me a ride?" Jen asked.

"Of course."

"Then it will work."

"Will you have any trouble getting out of the house?" Taryn asked her.

"I don't think so. It's Friday. I'll say I'm going to the movies with a friend and her big sister is picking me up."

***

The professor's house was several miles out of town. As the road grew darker and lonelier, Jen asked, "Are you sure this is the right way?"

"I think so," Taryn replied. "It's pretty much a straight shot until the turnoff on Route 10."

Sure enough, they came to the Route 10 sign and made the turn. A few minutes later, they arrived at the professor's house, which was at the end of a gravel lane. His house looked completely ordinary on the outside—white, two stories. The ordinariness surprised Jen, but what she had expected? Something from *The Jetsons? Stupid.*

Dr. Murphy met them at the door and ushered them into his home office. He didn't give them much chance to look around, but Jen noticed the inside of the house looked rather nondescript as well, save for a huge telescope by the large picture window in the living room.

His home office looked somewhat like his office at school, with a messy desk and a big whiteboard off to one side of it. The whiteboard, covered with complicated equations and drawings, made Jen's head ache.

She and Taryn sat on a black couch on the opposite side of the room from the desk, while the professor sat in his desk chair and turned to face them. As he sat, a large black cat jumped up into his lap. "Oh, I guess Shrodinger wants to join us," he said.

"Your cat is named Shrodinger?" Taryn asked.

"Yes, you know, Shrodinger's cat, the thought experiment . . ." he proceeded to tell them about the cat who was both dead and alive at the same time, when Taryn cut in.

"Dr. Murphy, I don't mean to be rude, but I already know about Schrodinger's cat, and Jen probably doesn't want to hear about it right now. We want to hear about your time travel."

"Of course. Well, in a sense, we're all time travelers . . ."

"Dr. Murphy—please!" Taryn was clearly running out of patience. Jen felt the same way, but wasn't about to upset the professor.

"All right, all right." The professor took his glasses off and started cleaning them with a handkerchief pulled from his pocket. A nervous affectation, Jen thought. "The short answer is yes. I am a time traveler."

With the secrecy and what he'd said in his office, this wasn't the shock it might have been. Still, it was hard to wrap her brain around it. "How do you do it?" Jen asked.

"Taryn, when you came in to talk to me a few days ago, you mentioned wormholes. That was a good guess. Through the use of a wormhole, I've been able to travel through time, as well as to parallel universes."

"So—how do you keep the wormhole from collapsing in on itself?" Taryn asked, sounding completely puzzled.

"I'm surprised you haven't figured that out already. Negative energy, of course."

"But how can you get enough?"

"I create it in my lab, but keeping the wormhole open requires far less negative energy than most people believe."

"Wow. . ."

"Pretty amazing, isn't it?"

In their excitement, both Taryn and the professor seemed to have forgotten Jen.

"I can't believe it. So it really is possible! You can travel to parallel universes too?"

"Yes. Actually, time travel is just a special case of traveling to a parallel universe. You're traveling to a universe very similar to ours, but in a different temporal location. Our universe is one of many, many universes."

Both Jen and Taryn gaped at him.

Finally Taryn said, "So if Jen wanted to go home, back to her original universe, could you send her there?"

The professor hesitated a long moment. Finally he said, "I could try. But I must warn you, Jen. If you wish to return, it could be dangerous."

"Dangerous how?" Jen failed to keep the quaver from her voice.

"Well, for starters, I've never had trouble with the wormhole collapsing in on itself. If I had, I wouldn't be standing here talking to you. I'd be dead. But I can't guarantee something wouldn't go wrong."

Jen gulped. *Going back could kill her?*

"And for another thing—"

"Isn't the possibility of death enough?" Jen tried for a bit of levity, but the attempt at humor fell flat.

The professor didn't smile. "Unfortunately, no. The other thing is I'm not sure I could send you to exactly the right place. You see, there are many universes out there, some quite different from ours, but others very similar. Some may be like this one, except you were never born. In others, a carbon copy of you might be living a life very similar to your adult life, but with some differences, like a different job. I could probably get you to a universe similar to the one you left, but in all likelihood it wouldn't be exactly the same."

"How do you figure out where to send me?" Jen asked. The information made her feel—homesick. That was the word. Sure, maybe she'd be better off here, starting over and making better choices. But not even having the option of going home . . .

"Well, since I've told you everything, I might as well show you my lab. But NO camera phones allowed. Place your phones on the table here, if you please." He looked at each of them sternly. Meekly, they complied.

Dr. Murphy's lab was at the back of his house. Several sophisticated-looking computers lined one wall, along with some high-tech electronic equipment unfamiliar to Jen. In the back was some machinery that sort of looked to Jen like pictures she'd seen of the Large Hadron Collider, though on a much smaller scale. In the middle of the room was a mysterious metal tube, extending from floor to ceiling, wide enough for a person. Jen and Taryn looked toward it questioningly.

"This is what I call the chamber," the professor said. He strode over to it and pressed a button. Part of the tube slid open to reveal a translucent, shimmery white light that appeared to be rotating around its width. The light was shot through with lines of color that gave it a circular structure.

"Don't get too close," the professor warned as the girls stepped closer. They immediately halted.

"What would happen if we did?" Jen had to ask, though she thought she knew.

"Well, you'd get sucked into the wormhole, and if I haven't plotted out your course ahead of time, who knows where you'd end up."

Both Jen and Taryn took several steps back.

"You don't need to be that far back," said the professor, chuckling for the first time that evening. "Remember, I was able to come close enough to the chamber to open it for you. I just didn't want you sticking your hands into the light or anything."

Jen and Taryn stood rooted to the spot. Jen figured Taryn's thinking was similar to hers. They were taking no chances.

Taryn asked, "You said, 'plotted your course.' How do you do that?"

The professor said, "Well, all this machinery—he nodded toward the machinery in the back of the room—and computing equipment helps me communicate with those in other universes. I've communicated with beings in advanced civilizations, beings who have traveled far more extensively throughout the multiverse than I have. They have helped advance my knowledge. I created the chamber and began traveling myself. I've been able to develop a rough map of the multiverse, part of it anyway, but I always send a message before traveling to any destination. Then I can refine my course, program it into the computer, and travel through the chamber."

Jen gaped at it, awestruck.

Taryn apparently recovered more quickly, though she, too, seemed stunned. "This is all so amazing!" She had begun walking around looking at all the equipment, but Jen was still rooted in place. She half-listened while Taryn and the professor talked about how everything worked.

Finally Taryn noticed her standing there. "Jen, are you all right? Maybe you should sit down." She led Jen over to a chair at one of the computers.

"I'm okay," Jen said as she sat down. "I just—" and she promptly burst into tears.

The professor seemed truly puzzled by her distress. "Aren't you excited about all this, my dear?"

"I think it's just a lot of information for her at once," Taryn said. "And she's been through a lot lately."

"She has," he agreed. He brought her a cup of water from the dispenser in one corner of the room.

"Thanks," Jen said shakily. She sipped, trying to compose herself.

"Feeling better?" Taryn asked.

"A little," said Jen. "It's just—I don't know whether I want to go home—go back—or not, but to think I might get killed trying, or get stuck somewhere awful . . ."

"Of course," Taryn said giving her a hug. "You're in a really tough spot."

When Jen looked up at the professor, he was glancing anxiously around the room, foot tapping. She figured he wasn't so much impatient as unaccustomed to dealing with emotional situations like this. "It's okay," she told him through her tears. "I'll be all right. I just need a little time to assimilate all this."

He cleared his throat. "I am hesitant to send you anywhere since this technology is so new, and for all the reasons I mentioned," he said. "But the decision is yours. I will help you if you want, as long as you understand the risks involved."

Jen nodded. "Thank you, Dr. Murphy. I need to think about it, if that's okay."

"Of course," he agreed. "With a decision of this magnitude, you should think it over very carefully. Take all the time you need, dear."

Chapter Thirteen

"I don't know what to do," Jen said to Taryn on the drive back. "This is unbelievable."

"Well . . ." Taryn hesitated. "I have no idea what I'd do either. But at least you *can* go back if you want."

"That's true," Jen agreed.

"You'll probably get an extra twenty-five years or so of life if you stay here," Taryn pointed out.

"Which would be awesome. And I'd never marry that asshole Josh."

"Do you think you'd still go into teaching?"

"Boy, I don't know." Jen sighed. "I enjoyed it well enough at first. But I'm kind of getting burned out. My classes are getting more and more crowded; I'm getting tired of spending my weekends grading; we got a pay cut recently due to funding; the politicians just want us to teach to the tests; it seems like things get worse and worse every year."

"That sucks."

"Yeah. Of course, it didn't help that I got so depressed when Josh left me. It probably wouldn't have mattered much what the job was at that point. I didn't want to do anything. I felt like—" Jen paused.

"Like?" Taryn prompted gently.

"Like I'd ruined everything," Jen said, fighting tears again.

"Jen, it's not your fault Josh is an asshole."

"Except part of me feels like maybe it is. Like if I'd been a better wife, if I'd just—been better, he wouldn't have found someone else." Jen thought she'd cried all she could over Josh, but now she burst into tears again.

Taryn slowed the car and turned into a mostly deserted McDonald's parking lot. She pulled into a parking spot and shut off the engine. She reached across the gearshift to give Jen an awkward hug. "Jen, you shouldn't blame yourself," she said softly. "You probably think I don't know anything, since I'm only twenty and have never been married. But I watched my parents go through this. And my mom blamed herself too. Dad left her and got remarried, and guess what? He cheated on his new wife, too. Some guys are just jerks. Including, I'm sorry to say, my dad."

"I'm sorry to hear that," Jen said. She had stopped crying, momentarily distracted from her own pain and feeling somewhat guilty. She, at least, had two wonderful parents.

"It's okay. I accepted it a long time ago. And he wasn't really that bad of a dad to me. I was just so mad at him for what he did to mom."

"I really wanted kids, but I guess it's a good thing we didn't have any yet Plenty of kids come through divorce just fine, but I'd hate to start out that way. Only now I'll probably never have any," Jen said sadly.

"Why not? You could stay here and have loads of time to find someone. Or even if you do go back, thirty-seven isn't exactly menopausal.'

"I know. I just feel like no one will ever want me again."

"Oh, come on. I'll bet you didn't even try dating after Josh left, did you?"

"No. I wasn't ready yet."

"Of course not. But someday you'll be ready, and I'll bet you'll find someone better. And I'll bet all the guys at your middle school have been checking you out here."

Jen flushed.

"I knew it. Is there someone in particular?"

"Taryn!" Jen blushed even harder. "I'm an adult. At least, emotionally if not physically."

"So there is someone."

"Well, kind of. A kid named Miguel. But—it's too weird. He's just a kid. And I still feel like I'm thirty-seven."

"Well, in a few years, you'll all be eighteen anyway," Taryn pointed out.

"Yeah, but I'd still feel a lot older than everyone else supposedly the same age. I suppose once I turn eighteen I could find someone several years older." Her parents wouldn't be thrilled if her eighteen-year-old self got together with someone in his mid-thirties or so, but Jen hoped they'd get past it.

"I guess you should take your time to decide," Taryn said.

Taryn was right. The enormity of the decision facing Jen was overwhelming.

***

She missed Lucy, especially on the bus and in art class. Lucy had texted her a couple of times, saying her new school didn't totally suck, high praise indeed from Lucy. She hadn't seen her mother yet, because family visits weren't allowed for the first 30 days in rehab. She hadn't complained about living with her aunt, but Jen supposed anything was better than living with her mom as long as the ex-boyfriend had been around.

Jen and Miguel had been eating lunch by themselves since Lucy had left, but about a week after her departure, Miguel said, "Let's go eat at that table." He indicated a table where a lot of his new jock friends sat.

Jen hesitated. "I don't know those kids." She instinctively wanted to avoid the popular kids who might be cruel. "But you go ahead," she said.

"Come on, Jen, you don't want to sit here by yourself," Miguel protested.

"It wouldn't be any big deal," she insisted.

"No, really, Greg invited both of us to eat with them when I saw him at track practice yesterday," Miguel said. "It won't be weird. Now come on." He took hold of her arm and started guiding her in the direction of the popular kids' table.

Jen considered arguing further, but decided against it. Miguel didn't want to leave her to eat alone, and of course he wanted to eat with his friends. She didn't want to make him choose. *This has to be the first time I've been invited to eat at the popular kids' lunch table.*

Everyone at the table acted like they knew Jen, not well, but who she was at least. She actually knew most of them too, but not necessarily because she'd come into contact with them in this universe. A few of them she'd taught as seventh graders. Patrick Davis, who'd commented on Miguel's note on her first day and led to her swearing and getting detention, was one of them. He was a class-clown type, not stuck up. Jen noted that Brianna sat at this table, but fortunately at the other end, where the cheerleaders clustered together. She thought Brianna gave her the stink eye as she sat down, but she ignored her. Maybe she was just being paranoid anyway. She and Miguel were sitting by mostly boys, except for a couple of girls, Isabel and Anna, who weren't cheerleaders. They were on the track team and student council. Both had been her students the year before. They were great kids and very popular, but Jen figured they didn't really fit in with Brianna and her snotty friends. They greeted her by name, but that didn't surprise her too much since they had some classes with her.

Isabel and Anna were talking about student council elections, which were coming up in a few weeks. "You should run for office, Jen," Isabel said.

"Uh, what?" Jen gaped at her.

"You should run for student council representative," Isabel said again.

"Yeah, you should, Jen," Anna chimed in. "You're way smarter and more mature than a lot of the other jerks who are running."

"Wow—thanks. But, uh, not many people know me yet. I mean I just moved here not too long ago. I don't think I'd win."

"But it's still a few weeks away," Isabel pointed out. "You'd have plenty of time to do some posters and you could do a Facebook page. We'd help you get lots of likes and spread the word. And everyone in band knows you." *Isabel knew she was in band?* "And Miguel knows all the jocks."

"I could be your campaign manager," Miguel said.

"Or you could run yourself," Jen pointed out.

"I'd rather stay behind the scenes," Miguel said. *Me too,* Jen thought.

"Just think about it," Isabel urged as the bell rang, signaling the end of the lunch period.

***

After lunch Jen had band. They were getting new music today. She hoped they'd get something challenging. She'd been practicing regularly since her arrival in this new universe— something she hadn't done in years. She had forgotten how much she enjoyed it.

Apparently chair placement auditions had been done shortly after Jen—or rather her alter-ego—had moved to Riverside. Her alter-ego had done a really good job and landed first chair. So her stomach dropped when she saw the huge flute solo in the new music.

"This is a tough solo, Jennifer, but I'm sure you're up for it," the band director said, smiling as he handed her the music.

Jen stared at the music in alarm. When she was hoping for challenging music, she hadn't meant she wanted a difficult solo. She'd been performing well enough since she'd been here, but a solo would likely expose her for the fraud she was.

"You look nervous," said Kristin Harper, who was second chair. She was first chair before Jen arrived—Jen had endured several snippy comments before figuring this out—and was not at all happy about Jen's getting the place she considered rightfully hers. "Listen, I'm used to doing solos. I can do it if you don't want to."

Jen gave her an incredulous look and said, "Nice try."

She supposed she should let the girl do it. After all, Jen already had her time to be in middle school band. But Kristin had pissed her off too much with her superior attitude. Jen refused to reward bad behavior. She ignored Kristin and studied the music, fingering the notes on her flute. It wasn't quite as hard as it looked, she thought with some relief.

Still, she was nervous when the band played the piece for the first time. When they got to her solo, she found herself suddenly short of breath. She breathed in quickly before she was supposed to start playing and managed not to start late. When she finished, she didn't even know if she'd done a good job or not, because she'd been so focused on getting through it without sounding terrible.

But when they finished the piece, the band director said, "Good job, Jen!" Jen beamed. The solo would be even better once she'd practiced. Even Kristin seemed impressed despite herself.

In her enrichment class, Amy made an announcement about a short story contest for eighth-graders that was coming up. Jen half-listened. Then Amy handed back corrected essays from the previous week. Jen saw the big red "A" as Amy set hers down. "You should enter the short story contest," she whispered to Jen. "You're a great writer."

The suggestion stunned Jen. And the idea made her a little uncomfortable. Should she really compete against a bunch of eighth-graders? Was that fair? At least in band, an eighth-grade version of herself had gotten first chair in the first place, which was why she got the solo.

But she ended up having no choice anyway. The next day in her Language Arts block, Amy made another announcement.

"I've decided to have you all write a story for the short story contest," she said. The contest was free to enter. Ignoring a few groans, Amy gave the class part of their block with her to start working on rough drafts.

Jen heard pencils scratching against paper as kids brainstormed ideas for their stories, but she was drawing a blank. She sat there for maybe fifteen minutes before an idea finally dawned on her. Why not write a science fiction story based on her experience? It would actually be kind of fun and would help her process the whole thing. She started jotting down some thoughts.

A few minutes before class ended Amy approached Jen's desk and looked at her notes. She asked Jen a couple of questions and said, "Sounds like a really interesting idea, Jen. When you get to high school you should write for the literary magazine. They do poems and short stories in a lot of different genres."

"Uh—that might be fun," Jen stammered. She couldn't quite wrap her brain around planning for high school.

"Think about it," said Amy as she walked away.

The feeling she'd had yesterday returned. Probably lots of kids wrote for the literary magazine. But would she be denying some kid a shot at their preferred college because she was writing for the literary magazine and not them? It would be kind of a big deal as far as extra-curricular activities went, and if her work was featured, it would mean less room for someone else.

And of course she should be writing better than a bunch of thirteen- and fourteen-year-olds. She may not have gotten her master's, but she did have a college degree, and she taught seventh-grade English.

Even though she'd have to get into a good college too if she stayed here, it seemed unfair.

When she got home, she called Taryn.

"I understand what you're saying," Taryn said after Jen had described her day. "But lots of people have unfair advantages for one reason or another. Nothing is ever all equal, no matter how hard people try to make things fair."

"I guess that's true," Jen agreed. "But still . . ."

"I doubt some kid isn't going to get into the college they want because of any one thing you do," Taryn said.

"Yeah, but if I stay, am I going to go through my whole life feeling like I cheated if I win at something?"

"You might. But wouldn't it get better as you get older? Then at least you'd be competing with other adults in whatever you did."

"Better than competing with kids," Jen agreed. "But I'd still have almost twenty-five years of extra life experience on anyone else my age."

"Right, but you're not always competing with people who are the same age in the workplace anyway," Taryn reminded her.

"True." But she didn't feel any better when she got off the phone. *Maybe I should go back,* she thought.

Chapter Fourteen

By the next morning, though, she wasn't so sure. Taryn was right. Nothing was ever totally fair. She felt uncomfortable now, but things would be pretty good in a few years. And if she stayed here, she'd have an extra twenty-five years of life!

This thought remained with her through the morning, even during her Language Arts block, when Amy urged her again to consider writing for the literary magazine in high school. Jen said again that she'd think about it.

At lunch, Isabel and Anna asked her about Seattle. "Was it awesome living there?" Isabel wanted to know.

"It was okay. I didn't know anything else." Jen hoped they didn't ask her anything she couldn't fake her way through.

"I'll bet it's soooo boring here for you," Anna said. "*I'm* bored and I've never lived anywhere else. There's nothing to do here."

Jen shrugged. "Riverside is okay."

"But Miguel said you had a boyfriend there," Isabel said. "Don't you miss him? Or did you guys break up?"

Damn, she'd forgotten all about her alleged boyfriend. She couldn't believe Miguel had actually told them that.

"No—we're still together. We text and talk on the phone a lot." Jen forced a smile.

Isabel wouldn't let the matter drop. "But that's not the same as being able to see each other."

"No, but my family will probably go to Seattle for a few days this summer. We can see each other then."

"But summer's *so far away*," Isabel complained. "How do you stand it?"

"Well, if it's true love, I guess it's worth it, right?" Anna asked. "Even if it's kinda tragic, with you guys being separated and all." She sighed at the romance of it.

"Oh, it's definitely true love, isn't it, Jen?" Miguel cut in, grinning at her.

She glared at him. While not malicious, he did seem to be enjoying her discomfort.

"It *is* true love, and we're both going to the University of Washington, so in a few years we can be together."

"You really think you're still going to be together by college?" Isabel seemed appalled by the idea. "And how do you even know where you want to go yet?"

"I know where I want to go," Anna said. "I want to go to the University of Hawaii. Where it's warm and sunny all the time. And really different from here."

"That would be great," said Isabel. "We should go there together! Awesome!"

Jen breathed a sigh of relief as the subject of the conversation turned away from her. But she still felt rattled and upset.

"Why did you tell them I have a boyfriend in Seattle?" she asked Miguel as they left the cafeteria and Isabel and Anna drifted out of earshot.

"I didn't think you'd be upset," Miguel said defensively. "They thought we were, you know, together, since we always eat together, and I told them we're just friends. They said we'd make a cute couple—hey, they said it, not me—so I told them you have a boyfriend. Was it a secret or something? Lucy knew."

"No, it's just . . ." Just what? That she already felt like a fraud and the boyfriend conversation had made it worse?

"Are you mad at me?" Miguel asked when she didn't complete her thought.

"No, I'm not mad. Don't worry." It wasn't Miguel's fault she had lied. She smiled at him.

"You sure?" he asked, looking worried.

"Yes, I'm sure. Really." She smiled again.

No, she wasn't mad, but the whole incident had helped her make a decision.

When she got home, she'd get in touch with Taryn and the professor and tell them she wanted to go back to her original universe.

***

"I feel like I'm always lying or pretending to be something I'm not," Jen explained to Taryn on the phone that afternoon. "Or even cheating, like with the short story contest. And things would get better later, but still—I can't tell anyone but you about growing up in Montana in the 80s—basically my whole life up to this point never existed. So even though I have good reasons to stay, I think I want to try to go back. Even though it's dangerous and I won't get twenty-five extra years of life."

"Well, I understand," Taryn said. "I have to say I'll really miss you, even though we've only known each other a little while," she said sadly. "I mean, you're not like anyone I've ever met before!" They both laughed.

"But I'm so excited about all the possibilities of time travel and other universes," Taryn continued. "I *have* to talk Dr. Murphy into letting me try it after you go back. After you get back safely, I think he might be more open to letting me try."

"Yeah, probably."

"Anyway, I'll call him right now and then call you back," Taryn said.

"I'll be waiting. And thanks. For all your help. I don't know what I would have done without you."

"It's been no problem at all. Like I said, it's all so exciting!"

***

Jen expected Taryn to call her right back. But fifteen minutes stretched into thirty, which stretched into an hour. What was taking so long? Maybe they were talking logistics. Or maybe Taryn was having trouble reaching the professor. She tried to do other things. She finished her homework, stupid, since she was leaving. At least it would be done for any alternate version of herself who returned in her place, as she figured would probably be the case.

Was that alter ego messing things up in *her* life? God, she hadn't even considered that. All the more reason to return as quickly as possible.

An hour and a half. How long could a logistics discussion take? Especially since she would need to be part of at least some of that discussion.

Nearly two hours had passed before Taryn finally called her back.

"Hey, what's up?" Jen asked. "Did you reach him? When can he do it?"

"Jen, something awful has happened," Taryn said. She sounded like she had been crying.

"Omigod, what?"

"Dr. Murphy's in the hospital. He had a heart attack. They don't think he's going to live!"

Two Months Later

Chapter Fifteen

The votes had been cast and tallied. The principal called Jen and the other student government candidates down to the office before making the official announcement of the winners over the intercom.

They'd done it. They won. Isabel was student body president for the freshman class of Riverside High next year. Miguel was vice president, and Jen was secretary-treasurer. Anna, whom Jen had tried to convince to run for a higher office, insisted she had too much else on her plate. She had run for, and won, a senate seat and had unofficially helped Isabel, Miguel, and Jen with their campaigns. Brianna had run against Jen and, certain Jen could never beat her, had neglected to campaign much. Jen grinned to herself as she noticed Brianna giving her the stink eye now.

And that wasn't the only good news. Jen had auditioned for and been accepted to the top high school band. She had also made the honor roll with straight As for third quarter. This last bit was less surprising than the first two things, though, since eighth-grade schoolwork failed to challenge her much. This had been true even the first time around.

Jen had accepted, albeit with some difficulty, that she was probably stuck here. The professor hadn't died. She and Taryn hadn't been able to visit him at the hospital as only family was allowed. But he'd had to have surgery and was on indefinite leave from the university. No one else could help her, as far as she and Taryn could determine. Though Dr. Murphy had shown Jen and Taryn the lab, neither of them had any idea of how anything worked. Plus, there would have been the small matter of getting his permission. The last time she'd spoken to Taryn, about a month ago, she'd told Jen she'd heard via the university grapevine that the professor might be moving into a nursing home near where his daughter lived in California. He may have done so by now.

The contact between Jen and Taryn had tapered off and then stopped completely. This was almost entirely Jen's fault. She realized Taryn was hurt by this, and she felt bad. But Jen thought it was easier to immerse herself in her new life rather than talking to Taryn about her old one. Also, Taryn had been a reminder that she'd lost an opportunity.

Lost opportunities. Everyone had them, but lost opportunities were way too much of a theme in her life lately.

She figured she had to immerse herself completely in her new life. She might as well make the most of her opportunity to start over.

Still, in her more reflective moments, she had to admit she missed her old, albeit messed-up life. She missed being able to talk to people about her real past before the last few months instead of having to remember her alter-ego's story and making things up.

Today was a happy day, though. She and her friends had overcome the odds and prevailed. She might have felt a little more guilty about denying someone else the opportunity to serve if that person hadn't been Brianna. She believed she was serving the greater good here. And Brianna hadn't been shut out of student government entirely; she was still a senator.

Taryn was right. It wasn't as though some kid wouldn't get in to the college of their choice because of any one thing Jen did.

"We should celebrate," Anna said as the four of them—Anna, Jen, Isabel, and Miguel—left the office after the official announcement. "Maybe we can go out for pizza tomorrow night or something."

"Sounds good," Miguel agreed. "You in, Jen?"

"Sure," said Jen.

Miguel had stopped hassling her to be more than friends, but they spent a lot of time together. She was sure he hadn't stopped thinking about it, but she couldn't do much about that. She had resolved not to date before she and her potential dates turned eighteen. The thought of it was just too icky. She'd deal with romantic relationships in college. She'd probably still feel a lot more mature than anyone she dated, but maybe being around younger people all the time would make her feel younger in some ways.

So when she got home later and checked her cell phone she was surprised to see a text from Taryn. It read: "Dr. Murphy coming back to work Monday."

Stunr.ed, Jen half sat, half fell onto her bed. Her jaw dropped. She hadn't even considered this possibility, not with the professor's age and health. She actually felt numb.

Once the feeling returned to her fingers, she texted back, "WHAT?!"

In response, her phone rang, Taryn's name popping up on the screen.

"He's really going back to work?" Jen asked as she answered the phone.

"I didn't believe it either at first," Taryn said. "I thought he was going into a nursing home, like I told you. When I heard otherwise, I thought it couldn't be true. But I checked with the main office in the physics department, and apparently he IS coming back."

"Wow."

"I know! It's crazy. I guess he refused to live with his daughter or go into a nursing home, and his doctor cleared him to come back to work, so . . . do you want to talk to him again about going back?"

"Wow, I don't know . . . I mean, this is really sudden . . . "

"Yeah, it's a shock," Taryn sympathized. "But I figured I should tell you. I mean, I figure if the professor's well enough to go back to work he'd be willing to help you."

"Yeah," Jen breathed. "I appreciate your calling. And, uh, I'm sorry I haven't been good about keeping in touch. I was so bummed; I mean, I'd decided to go back and then I was stuck here . . . But now, I'm kind of getting settled in, you know? Getting used to things. So I don't know what to do."

"It's a really hard decision," Taryn agreed. "I'm really not sure what I'd do either. But maybe I should talk to the professor and see if he's at least still willing to help before you get all tangled up in knots over it."

"Yeah, that's probably a good idea."

***

"What's wrong, Jen?" Miguel asked.

She, Miguel, Isabel, and Anna were at the pizzeria near the middle school. Jen tried to focus on her friends and having a good time, but her thoughts kept straying back to the decision she had to make. What should she do?

"Jen?" Miguel prompted, when she didn't answer him. "Earth to Jen!"

"Sorry," Jen said. "I was just thinking."

"Looks like it must have been about something pretty important," Miguel observed. Anna and Isabel stopped talking and stared at Jen, whose cheeks flushed.

So she smiled and shook her head. "I was thinking how awesome next year is going to be."

"It's going to be so much fun!" Anna exclaimed. "I can't wait."

Jen looked around the table at her friends. Would she be here next year? Should she stay around for next year? Would she regret it if she did? Theoretically she could change her mind if she decided to stay here, but as recent events proved, the professor wasn't getting any younger. If he agreed to help her now and she waited, she might miss her chance altogether.

"Jen, you're tuning out again," Miguel said.

"Oh, sorry, what?"

"I asked if everyone wanted to go to a movie," Isabel said. "Anna and Miguel do. Are you in? I can probably get my mom to drive us."

"Oh, sure." At least people wouldn't be expecting her to participate in conversation. "I'll call my mother and ask." She fished her cell phone out of her sweatshirt pocket.

***

After they'd gotten back from the movie, around 10:00 pm, Jen was alone in her room when her phone buzzed. She got her second surprise text of the day, this one from Lucy. "In front of ur house which rm is urs?"

She texted back, "WHAT?!"

Seconds later she got a reply. "Tell me which window 2 go to 2 & let me in!"

Not knowing what else to do and not wanting to take the chance Lucy might knock on the front door in desperation, she texted the instructions on how to get to her window. Unfortunately, it was not on the ground floor, but Lucy could climb the tree next to it.

"Lucy, what's going on?" Jen asked when Lucy was safely inside. "Why are you here?"

"Manny found me," Lucy said urgently.

"WHAT?"

"Look!" She showed Jen a text from Manny, which read, "B seeing u soon, hon."

Creepy.

"Well, but that doesn't mean he knows where you are," Jen pointed out. "He already had your phone number, right? Did you get a new cell phone when you moved to Seattle?"

"No, and yes, he had my number, but look at this," Lucy said, showing her the phone again.

Fearfully, Jen read the message. "U think u can hide at ur aunt's but u can't hide from me. C U soon in Seattle."

Okay, now she understood why Lucy was scared. But . . .

"Why didn't you tell your aunt about this?" Jen asked.

"I did! She told me not to worry. She said there's no way Manny knows where we live, even if he knows I live in Seattle now. She doesn't get it. Just because her phone number isn't listed doesn't mean he can't get our address. He's good at finding things out."

Jen considered what to say, *how can I possibly help?* being one of the chief possibilities. Lucy was right, though. If Manny— who had been kicked out of Lucy and her mother's house before any options for Lucy were discussed—had found out she was living with her aunt in Seattle, he probably knew or could find out the address.

"Maybe we should show this to my parents and they can call the police," Jen finally suggested. "Those texts sound pretty threatening to me. I can't believe your aunt would blow that off."

"I *told* my aunt to call the police, but she didn't think they would do anything. Well, not exactly. She thought we might be able to get a restraining order, but it might actually make things worse. The whole thing might just make him mad. She thought it would be best to leave it alone and we'd be all right. But I'm scared, Jen!" She clutched at Jen's arms. Jen had never seen her like this. Lucy didn't admit to fear easily.

"Well, I'm not sure what we should do," Jen admitted.

"Can I stay here?" Lucy implored.

"What? Stay here? My parents would never—"

"Just let me hide out in your room. Just for tonight. They'll never even know I'm here."

"Well, I don't think . . ."

"Please, Jen," Lucy begged. "I wouldn't ask, but it's important."

Jen conceded the point.

"Well, you can stay here tonight, I guess," she said. "But at least text your aunt and tell her you're okay."

"I can't! She might figure out where I am. Like, contact the phone company and see which cell phone tower it bounced off of."

"But, Lucy, she must be worried sick about you." And they could determine the approximate location of her phone even if she didn't make a call, but Jen decided not to remind Lucy of that.

"Maybe, but I tried to talk to her, and she wouldn't listen."

"Well—" what else could she say? Then she had an idea. "Where is your mother? Is she still in treatment?"

"She's in a halfway house for a little while. She'll come and live with my aunt and me soon. Why?"

"Well, have you talked to her about this?"

"Not really," Lucy admitted. "I mean, I think she has enough problems, and I only see her a couple times a week."

"Maybe you can text her, and she can contact your aunt."

"But they might still find me!"

"You don't think they'd think to check here anyway?"

"Well, if they'd think of it anyway, why should I text them?"

Jen sighed. It was getting late and she was tired. "Okay, fine," she said. You can stay here tonight. We can talk more in the morning."

"Thanks, Jen," Lucy said, her tone heartfelt. "I owe you one."

Jen got her sleeping bag out of her closet and tossed it to Lucy. "Put it down on that side of my bed," she said, pointing. "That way if my mom pokes her head in she won't see you." Lucy did as Jen asked without comment.

"Are you hungry?" Jen asked. "Do you need a snack?"

"That would be awesome," Lucy said. "Thanks."

Jen went to the kitchen and peered into the fridge, assessing her options. Leftover chicken, potatoes . . .

"Still hungry?"

Jen jumped at her mother's voice. "Oh, hi, mom." Did she sound guilty?

"I would have thought after pizza and snacks at the movies you'd be full," her mom said.

"Oh . . . teenagers," Jen said, smiling, hoping she sounded convincing. "We're always hungry."

"I guess so." Her mother laughed. "I wish I could still eat that way."

Me, too, Jen almost said, then caught herself. She loved her teenage metabolism.

She loaded food onto a plate, wishing her mother would leave the kitchen. But her mother was taking her time fixing herself a cup of Chamomile tea.

"Wow, you're having a whole other dinner," her mother observed, as Jen put a couple of pieces of chicken on a plate—one for herself and one for Lucy, but she couldn't very well use two plates—along with some potato salad. She also grabbed a bag of chips and two no-caffeine Pepsis, hoping her mother wouldn't say anything about her taking two cans. She grabbed a couple of spoons for the potato salad while her mother wasn't looking, and some napkins.

"I told you—teenagers are always hungry. And I didn't eat much at the movies. 'Night, mom!" she called as she headed up the stairs.

"'Night, hon," her mother called back. Jen breathed a sigh of relief. She carefully balanced everything and quickly opened her door.

"Awesome!" Lucy said as soon as she shut the door. "Was that your mother I heard you talking to?" she asked as they started to eat.

"Yeah."

"Was she suspicious of how much food you took and the two sodas?"

"I don't think she noticed I took two sodas or two spoons. I tried to make sure she wasn't paying attention when I did. I kept wishing she'd leave the damned kitchen, but she took forever to make herself a cup of tea. But she did comment on how I was fixing myself another dinner when I'd had pizza and then snacks at the movies. I just reminded her teenagers are always hungry."

"Especially me. I haven't eaten since I left my aunt's house this morning."

"How did you get here, anyway?" Jen wondered why the question had not occurred to her sooner.

"I 'borrowed' some of my aunt's grocery money and bought a bus ticket."

"Lucy!"

"Hey, I was desperate. Besides, it's not like my aunt is hurting for money."

"So how did you get to the bus station from here?" The city buses would have stopped running by then.

"By cab. I had the driver drop me off a block away from your house so as not to tip off your parents."

"How did you get my address?" Jen was surprised by this, and that Lucy would even care where she lived. Once upon a time, they might have exchanged addresses so they could write to each other, but in this day and age, they just had each other's cell phone numbers and email addresses, and they were friends on Facebook.

However, the Internet also made it easier to find people.

"I remembered you saying your dad teaches at the high school and your parents are still together, so I got on the website for the high school and found one teacher with the last name of Edwards. I figured that must be him. You guys kind of look alike, too. So that's how I got his first name, and then I found him in the white pages."

"Oh."

"You don't want me here," Lucy said sadly, with a touch of bitterness.

"It's not that," Jen said. "I'm glad to see you again, even if the circumstances aren't good. It's just that I'm not sure how to help you. I mean, I can't hide you here forever, and I'm sure my parents won't let you stay here without contacting your aunt, who probably wouldn't agree to it. And even if she did, who's to say Manny wouldn't come here?"

"He probably will try to find me in Riverside when he doesn't find me in Seattle. But that's okay. Don't worry about your parents finding out. He won't come to your house; he doesn't know who you are. It was different with my aunt since he knew my mom's family and everything. But I plan to be long gone soon."

Jen's stomach dropped. "Where are you going?"

Lucy hesitated. "You won't like it."

"Try me."

"I have a boyfriend in Spokane. He's eighteen and has his own place. He said I could stay with him."

Oh, dear God. Jen struggled to keep any shock or disapproval out of her voice. She had to stay calm or Lucy would clam up. "Are you sure that's a good idea, Lucy? I mean, how did you meet this guy?"

"Online, of course. He's really nice."

"Have you actually met him in person?"

"Well, no, but we chat all the time on Facebook, and we've talked on the phone. See?" Lucy showed her a picture on her phone. "That's him."

The guy looked like a thug to Jen, with multiple tattoos and a sneering expression.

"But, Lucy, he could really get into trouble for being with someone underage," Jen pointed out. "You don't want that to happen, do you?"

"He's got a fake ID for me," Lucy said, as if that solved everything. "And if Manny finds me, Raton will kick his ass."

Rat? Really? So that was it. Lucy felt she would be safe with Raton. "But what makes you so sure he is who he says he is? He might end up being a lot like Manny."

"Oh, please," Lucy scoffed. "You're such a worrier, Jen. I told him about Manny and he thinks Manny's an asshole. He even said he'd kick Manny's ass if he ever came near me again. And do you really think he made up his whole Facebook profile?"

"Well, it wouldn't be hard to do," Jen said. "People lie about themselves on the Internet all the time." *Plus, even if he'd been completely honest, the truth was bad enough.*

"But on Facebook he's friends with people he went to school with and works with. Wouldn't they know if he was lying about something and say something about it?"

"Maybe, but who knows what his friends are like? Besides, all they know is information he shares with all his friends, not things he says when he chats with you."

"It'll be fine," Lucy insisted. "Don't make me sorry I told you. Not everyone has a perfect home life like you."

"I understand," Jen said sympathetically. "I really do. But didn't you have a pretty good deal going at your aunt's? You were going to a private school and away from Manny and your mom was getting treatment. Couldn't you just be careful and keep an eye out for him?"

"You don't get it! I can't stay in Seattle if Manny's there."

Jen reluctantly decided to let the subject drop, realizing the discussion made Lucy angry. At least she had some time to figure out what to do.

"Okay, Lucy, I get it," she said. Then, so Lucy wouldn't be too suspicious, she added, "Just be careful, okay?"

"I will," Lucy said, softening slightly. "You don't need to worry so much."

Yeah, right.

"How are you getting to Spokane?" Jen asked.

"By bus. I'll leave here in the morning. You won't have to worry about your parents finding me."

Jen thought about that. Lucy would need to take a city bus to the bus station, unless she wanted to walk all the way there, which Jen doubted. City buses on Saturdays started running at about 9:00 am. So she'd have to act before then if she didn't want Lucy to run off to Spokane and into the arms of Raton.

Jen could see Lucy was getting tired. "You can use my bathroom to wash up and everything. Be sure and lock the door on my sister's side in case she wakes up and needs to use it."

After they settled down for the night, Lucy fell asleep quickly. Jen wondered how she could fall asleep so quickly with her future in tatters. But, Lucy had gone through a lot of emotional exhaustion, plus bus trips took longer than car trips because the bus stopped everywhere.

When she was sure Lucy was asleep, Jen pulled Lucy's phone out from under her pillow. She had found it in Lucy's backpack while Lucy was in the bathroom. Now she stole out of bed and into the bathroom, quietly shutting the door behind her. She sat down on the closed toilet lid and scrolled through Lucy's contacts. When she found the one she wanted, she began a new text and started typing.

Chapter Sixteen

"But she can't be here." A groggy Jen heard her mother talking and footsteps on the stairs.

"I'm telling you, it said in the text I got that she IS here." Jen didn't recognize the second voice calling from the bottom of the stairs.

"Let me ask Jen, but I'm sure—"

Jen eyed her bedside clock blearily. Five-thirty a.m. Crap! She sat up. Lucy's aunt must be here. She'd wanted to be up and dressed first, and be able to explain things to her parents ahead of time, though she'd had little idea of what she'd say.

Her mother knocked softly on her door. "Jen, hon, I'm sorry to wake you, but—"

Eying the closed door with dread, Jen said, "Come on in, mom."

Last night she had texted Lucy's aunt. In the text she told her where Lucy was and explained Lucy's fear of Manny and the texts Lucy had received from him. She said she assumed Selena, Lucy's aunt, understood the situation, but it might be best to get a restraining order if possible so Lucy would feel safer. She urged Selena to hurry to Riverside, before Lucy went to Spokane to meet up with a guy who called himself "Raton."

After sending her texts, she had turned off Lucy's phone and put it back in her backpack. Even if Lucy hated her for squealing, Jen couldn't let her run off to Spokane.

She had assumed Lucy's aunt was awake and had her phone close by, and she had figured correctly that Selena would leave for Riverside right away. But she hadn't thought she would fall asleep, so she'd figured she would have plenty of time to get up and dressed before Lucy's aunt arrived, and she'd have time to wake her parents.

"Honey, a lady named Selena Gomez is here." Confusion colored her mother's words. She was dressed in a bathrobe and had a severe case of bedhead. "She says you texted her in the middle of the night and said her niece is here?" Her mother couldn't see Lucy on the other side of Jen's bed, or things would have been cleared up without asking.

"Mom—" Jen began.

But before she could say anything else, Lucy stirred and said, "What's going on—"

Jen's mother stepped further into the room. "Is this her?"

"Omigod!" Too late, Lucy burrowed into her sleeping bag.

"Jen, what is going on here?"

"Mom, I was going to tell you—"

"Is she here?" a voice called from downstairs, followed by footsteps storming up the stairs. "Lucy—"

Lucy emitted a groan from within her sleeping bag.

"Mom, I was going to tell you," Jen said again.

"Do you mean to tell me this girl stayed over and I knew nothing about it?" her mother demanded.

"Well, it was sort of an emergency, and I was going to tell you."

"Lucy! Where are you?" Now Lucy's aunt was also at Jen's bedroom door.

Jen pointed to the floor on the other side of her bed. Her mother and Lucy's aunt walked around it and saw Lucy, or rather, a vaguely Lucy-shaped lump in the sleeping bag.

Lucy's aunt bent over and picked up one end of the sleeping bag and shook it slightly. "Come on, Lucy. The jig is up."

Lucy poked her head out of her sleeping bag, shooting a glare in Jen's direction. Jen winced. Anger poisoned the silence.

Finally, Jen's mom broke it by saying, "Just what is going on here? Did this girl—Lucy—really stay here all night?"

"Yes," Jen said. Both her mother and Lucy's aunt turned to stare at her. She could still feel Lucy's glare. "Sorry," she said, to no one in particular. "Lucy texted me after I got home from the movies. She took the bus from Seattle—"

Aunt Selena cut in. "On the bus? Lucy, where did you get the money?"

Lucy glared again at Jen, then turned to her aunt. "From the grocery money you keep in the cookie jar." Her tone was unrepentant.

"You took all that? Never mind—we'll talk about that later, *including* how you're going to pay me back. Right now I want to know what you were thinking."

Lucy glowered at her aunt. "I was *thinking* I didn't want to be around when Manny decided to visit us. And you weren't a whole lot of help, so I decided to go to someone who would be."

"Jen, we should leave so they can talk," Jen's mother broke in.

"Hand me my robe, will you?" Jen asked. She was totally fine with leaving the room.

"No, actually, I'd like to hear what Lucy told you," Aunt Selena said to Jen.

Jen glanced uncomfortably from the scowling Lucy to her mother, whom she hoped would save her. No such luck. Quite the opposite, in fact. "Yes, Jen, you started to tell us what happened."

Jen sighed. Lucy was already mad at her and would probably never speak to her again, so she supposed it didn't matter what she said. "She texted me and said she was in town and close to my house and asked which window was mine. I told her and she came in through the window—"

"Through the window?" her mother asked. "She climbed up the tree?"

Jen nodded.

"She could have fallen and been hurt!" her mother admonished.

"Mom, it's not that high," Jen said. And it was kind of beside the point now anyway. She tried to move things along. "Lucy mentioned not wanting to be in Seattle because of Manny. She's terrified of him. Maybe . . . you might reconsider the restraining order idea?"

"Thanks, but I'll handle this," Lucy's aunt said severely.

Well, maybe she shouldn't have tried to give advice so soon, but Jen wondered why Selena even asked her for information. She hadn't told her anything she hadn't already said when she'd contacted her in the middle of the night. Thinking over what she'd texted, she supposed she'd sounded rather adult, and it may have seemed disrespectful considering she was only supposed to be thirteen. She had made every attempt to be polite and not overstep, but even so.

In any case, even though her mother was mad at Jen also, she didn't appreciate Selena's tone. "Well, maybe you should handle it elsewhere then. Even though she was horribly misguided and I still don't understand quite what happened, it does sound like Jen was trying to help."

"Fine. I apologize for the disruption to your family, and I do appreciate your daughter's letting me know where Lucy was," Selena said in a somewhat more conciliatory tone. "What my niece doesn't quite seem to realize, though, is that running off is hardly going to keep her safe. If anything, my sister's loser boyfriend is more likely to be here than in Seattle, no matter what he texted to Lucy."

Jen agreed with Selena there. Lucy wasn't safer on her own, and Manny was from here and likely to return at some point. Still, though, she doubted Selena grasped the gravity of the situation. Lucy didn't feel safe. Until she did, she might very well run off again. Jen wished right now she could talk to Selena from an educator's perspective, rather than another kid.

And Lucy was unconvinced. "You don't know him like I do," she said to her aunt.

"That may be, but we can't impose on these people any longer. We have several hours on the ride home to discuss it. You've got five minutes to get ready."

Lucy didn't budge for a moment, and Jen thought that she might actually refuse to go with Selena. But eventually she crawled out of her sleeping bag, grabbed her backpack, and went into the bathroom, slamming the door behind her.

An awkward silence filled the room after she left.

"I'm so sorry for all the trouble," Selena finally said.

"Well—teenagers, you know," Jen's mother said uncomfortably. "Would you prefer to wait downstairs? You'd be more comfortable."

"Thank you, yes," Selena said.

Jen watched them go with a sigh of relief. She was sure her mother would have plenty to say to her later, though. She sat in bed, frozen, until Lucy emerged from the bathroom. "Lucy—" she started to say.

Lucy's hate-filled glare stopped her short. Jen couldn't find her voice for a moment. She tried again. "Lucy, I—"

"Don't ever fucking speak to me again!" Lucy slammed the door as she left.

Stunned, Jen almost didn't notice the timid knock on the door between her room Melanie's. "Jen?"

"Melanie?" Of course. No one could have slept through all this. She was surprised Lucy hadn't found her listening at the door when she went in there.

Melanie cautiously opened the door. "She's gone; you can come in," Jen told her.

"What the hell happened?"

"It's a long story." Jen's sudden fatigue reminded her of the early hour. "I'm sorry we woke you up."

"What happened?" Melanie asked again.

"Why don't we start with what you heard? It might save me some time."

"Lucy snuck in last night and stayed over, and she ran away from Seattle because of some dude named Manny."

"Well, then you pretty much understand what happened." Jen wished she could talk to Melanie for awhile and not face her mother. Actually, she wanted to go back to sleep, but that wasn't going to happen. The front door had slammed shut downstairs— Lucy and her aunt leaving, she assumed, and she heard her mother's feet on the stairs now.

Chapter Seventeen

So Lucy went back to Seattle with her aunt and Jen was grounded indefinitely. Jen's parents sympathized with her desire to help her friend, but had major problems with her methods. They did admit Jen had done the right thing in notifying Lucy's aunt, but were upset Lucy had stayed overnight without their knowledge. So Jen was grounded until her parents decided otherwise.

They should be grateful I didn't have a boy in the room, Jen thought. Pointing this out would hardly help her case, though.

While her parents agreed that a restraining order against Manny might be a good idea, they refused to talk to Lucy's aunt about it as Jen had asked. It's not our business, they'd said. Lucy's aunt was aware of the situation and Jen's parents believed Selena would take appropriate measures to ensure Lucy's safety.

While Jen believed Selena cared about Lucy's safety, her parents' words failed to reassure her. She doubted Selena had ever dealt with someone like Manny.

Of course, restraining orders didn't always work anyway.

This was definitely a time to hate being a kid. She couldn't have told Selena what to do even if she'd met her as an adult, but she might have had some influence as an educator as opposed to a thirteen-year-old child.

Taryn had texted her and said the professor was willing to help her. Jen said it would probably have to wait, since she was grounded at the moment. Taryn had pointed out she could just pick Jen up from school. Jen said she'd think about it.

But since then, her parents had decided mere grounding wasn't enough, and took away her phone and computer.

She remained in a state of limbo, going to class, coming home, doing her homework. If she needed a computer for homework, she had to use her laptop under the supervision of one of her parents.

She was slowly going crazy.

School was her only reprieve. At least there she could talk to Miguel and her other friends. She told Miguel what had happened with Lucy, but she didn't tell her other friends. No sense in getting the rumor mill started again. She tried emailing Lucy from the computer lab at school, but Lucy never answered her. Though this didn't surprise Jen, it did upset her.

A couple of weeks after her eventful weekend with Lucy, there was a big announcement along with the usual morning updates over the intercom. The results were in for the eighth-grade short story contest. They announced the second-, third-, and fourth-place winners. And then they revealed the first place winner—Jennifer Edwards!

"Congratulations, Jen!" Amy said to her.

"Awesome, Jen!" Miguel whispered, reaching out from his desk across the aisle to pat her shoulder.

Jen realized she shouldn't be surprised. She'd been competing against a bunch of eighth-graders. But somehow the news still stunned her. Even though she had taught language arts, it had been a long time since she had written a short story, for one thing. And for another, she'd made a deliberate attempt to not turn in her very best work, out of guilt.

And she did feel guilty. She'd gotten a hundred-dollar gift certificate to a bookstore in town and a scholarship to a summer writing workshop. She'd beaten out a bunch of kids to get those prizes.

"You don't seem very excited," Miguel observed as they left class later.

"Well, I'm happy, I guess." Jen groped for words. "I guess . . . I just think there are kids out there who are a lot more deserving."

"What? Why would you think that?"

"Oh, I don't know. I guess I'm being weird and random." She smiled at Miguel. "Don't pay any attention to me."

***

It was May now and spring fever struck the students of Riverside Middle School. The kids at Jen's lunch table discussed summer plans. Anna was taking a trip to Hawaii with her family. Isabel had a summer babysitting job. Miguel wasn't sure of his plans yet.

"We traveled around Spain all of last summer," he said. "This will be my first summer in the States for awhile."

"Are you going to take any kind of trip?" Anna asked, high with thoughts of Hawaii.

"Probably, but I don't know where yet," he replied. He turned to Jen. "What about you? Are you going anywhere this summer?"

"I don't know," Jen said. She had no idea at all. Her parents hadn't said anything about vacation plans. Wistfully, she remembered her childhood summers in Montana, when she and her family had gone to Glacier Park for a few days every summer.

"I can ask around if you want a babysitting job," Isabel said.

"I'm not sure yet. Can I let you know in a few days?" If she stayed, she might need something to do.

"Sure, no prob."

It made her sad to realize how little she could share with anyone. She couldn't tell anyone about her Montana summers because supposedly she lived in Seattle until a few months ago. She couldn't even talk to her *family* about her life experiences, even though in her mind she'd shared many of these experiences with them. It was almost as if she hadn't existed until two and a half months ago. She hadn't gotten used to that, even now that she had more experiences in this world. She supposed over the years, if she stayed here, it would get easier, but not for quite awhile yet.

    ***

When Jen and Melanie got home from school, their mother was already there. "What's going on?" Jen asked immediately. Her mother never came home early.

"Well, hopefully nothing," her mother said. She told Jen and Melanie to sit down. "I heard from Lucy's aunt a couple of hours ago," she began. "She called and asked if Lucy had shown up here."

"What? Lucy's not even talking to me," Jen said. "She's really mad at me because I ratted her out to her aunt the first time." She paused as she considered her mother's words. "So Lucy's missing again?" She felt a flutter of fear in her gut for Lucy. Something told her this disappearance might not be of her own volition.

"Yes, she's gone. I told her aunt I doubted she was here, but I got someone to cover for me and came home to check—"

This made no sense to Jen. Even if Lucy did return, Jen would hardly have brought her here during the school day. But maybe her mother thought they'd assume the house would be empty . . .

"She'd never come back here," Jen said.

"That's what I figured, but her aunt was practically hysterical. I'm sorry, but I checked your phone to make sure she hadn't left you a message."

"I'm sure she didn't," Jen said. "How long has Lucy been gone?" This didn't sound good, but Lucy might have just ditched school with a friend or something.

"You're right, she didn't leave you a message. Apparently she never got to school this morning," her mother said. "Her aunt says she watched her get on the city bus this morning to go to school. The stop is less than a block from her house. But then the school called this afternoon, saying Lucy hadn't shown up at all today. So something happened between the time she got on the bus and the time she should have arrived at school."

Jen's heart sank. Lucy had already been missing for several hours. "I hate to ask an obvious question, but did her aunt check with Lucy's friends and all that?" Jen asked.

"Yes, and none of them saw her at all today either."

"Oh no." Jen felt lightheaded. "I'll bet Manny took her."

"We don't know that," her mother said quickly.

"Yes we do," Jen moaned. If only the adults had listened to her and Lucy. The end result might have been the same, but maybe not.

"Well, we shouldn't panic yet. Her aunt is still calling some people she knew here—"

"Mom, she needs to call the police! I know she's only been missing for a few hours, but with Manny out there . . . " Jen didn't need to finish her thought.

"Yes, I'll call her back now. She just wanted to check with Lucy's friends before calling the police."

So after Jen's mom called Lucy's aunt, Selena called the police, and an Amber Alert was issued. Jen felt marginally better, but she still believed a lot of time had been wasted. Her mom told her to try not to worry, but seemed unconvinced by her own words.

"Is Lucy going to be okay?" Melanie asked Jen later that evening, when Jen was making an attempt at homework.

"I hope so," Jen said.

"Do you really think her mom's old boyfriend took her?"

Jen regarded her sister. Would too much honesty scare her? "I'm not sure," she said finally. "I hope she just went off with some friends, but it doesn't sound like it. Her aunt has pretty much checked with everyone."

"She ran away before," Melanie pointed out. "And she came here."

"Well, she won't this time. She kind of hates me now for telling her aunt where she was."

"But maybe she ran away again and went to another friend. Or a boyfriend. Didn't you say she had a boyfriend in Spokane?"

"Yes, she might have done that." Jen wasn't sure what was worse, Manry taking her or her going to stay with the boyfriend in Spokane.

***

Seeing Jen worry so much about her friend must have made her parents decide she'd suffered enough. They gave her her phone and computer back and said she was ungrounded, as long as she promised to tell them immediately if she heard from Lucy at all. Jen agreed without complaint. She wished hearing from Lucy was even a remote possibility.

Sleep eluded Jen that night. After tossing and turning for hours, she got up and went downstairs to the kitchen. She doubted warm milk would help, but it was worth a try. Sitting at the kitchen table drinking it, she heard light footsteps on the stairs.

"Jen, what are you doing up?" her mother asked from the doorway of the kitchen.

"I couldn't sleep," she answered, indicating the glass of milk.

"I know you must be worried sick about Lucy."

"Yeah. I just wish her aunt had listened to me when I said she should get a restraining order."

Her mom came over and put an arm around her. "Maybe she should have. But you don't know that would have changed anything. Restraining orders don't always work. So I hope you aren't feeling bad because she didn't listen to you."

"She would have listened to me if I weren't a kid."

"Well, maybe. But you can't do anything about that. You tried to be a good friend to Lucy. That's all you could have done."

"I guess."

"It's true. Now you should try and get some sleep."

***

Back upstairs, her mother's words reverberated in her head; in particular, the words "You can't do anything about that," since it obviously wasn't true. When she finally fell asleep, she dreamed Manny held Lucy captive in a small, dark cave. Jen observed the scene, apparently invisible. She had never met Manny, but in the dream he was huge, hulking, and angry. This was pretty unimaginative of her subconscious, Jen supposed. He was yelling something at Lucy, but slurring his words as if very drunk, so much so that Jen couldn't understand him. Lucy cowered silently in a corner at first, but then she stood up and yelled at Manny, "I just want my life back!"

Jen woke up then, sweating and shaking. She glanced at the clock. 6:05 am. It was almost time to get up anyway. She was deciding whether it would be worth it to try and get a little more sleep or if she should just get up when the hallway door opened.

"Mom," she said, startled.

"Oh! Sorry," her mom said. "I didn't knock because I thought you'd still be asleep. I just wanted to tell you they found Lucy and Manny."

"They did? Great! Where? Is she okay?"

"She's okay. They stopped somewhere in California. Manny was getting gas and Lucy managed to alert somebody that she needed help. I'm not exactly sure what happened. Her aunt just called. But Manny was planning on taking her to Mexico. He has family there.'

"Oh, my God!"

"Yeah. But he won't be getting out of jail anytime soon, with charges of kidnapping and transporting a minor across state lines. Plus, he'll be considered a flight risk, so I can't imagine any judge would let him out on bail."

"Well, that's good."

"Yeah. Hey, you can stay home from school if you want. I know you didn't sleep well last night."

"Actually, I think I will. I'm really tired."

Assured of Lucy's safety, Jen slept soundly and dreamlessly for a couple of hours. She awoke at 10:00 am to a silent house. Everyone was at work or school.

Now she finally had a chance to think clearly, and she made a decision.

Her phone sat on her nightstand. She took it and texted Taryn:

We need to talk.

Chapter Eighteen

"So you're sure?" Taryn asked her.

"Yes," said Jen. They were sitting across from each other at a table in the student union. Jen's mother thought she was at Anna's.

"Not to be nosy or anything, but can I ask why you're so sure now when you weren't before?"

"I just—things that happened in the past few days made me decide I don't want to stay here."

"Really? Like what?" Taryn asked, her brow furrowed in concern.

"Well—I won a short story contest."

"You did? But that's great. Congratulations."

"Thanks, but remember what we talked about?"

"You mean about your competing against 'real' eighth-graders?"

"Yeah."

"Well, didn't we decide it's unlikely that any one thing you do will have a huge effect on someone else, like cause them not to get into the college they want? You're not even in high school yet."

"Right, but—I'm still cheating. It doesn't feel right. And something happened to a friend of mine." She told Taryn about Lucy. "I felt so helpless. And I was so frustrated when people refused to listen to me. The next several years would be like that."

"I'm sorry about your friend," Taryn said. "That's awful. But you probably wouldn't be in an extreme situation like that very often."

"I know," Jen sighed. "And even if I'd been talking to her and her aunt as an educator, they still might not have listened to me. But I'd still have several years of frustration. And . . ." she hesitated.

"What?" Taryn asked when the silence lengthened.

"Well, this is kind of related to the cheating feeling, but it's worse than that. I—I feel like an imposter in my own life. Like I didn't exist before I came to this universe. I can't share any of my history with anyone except you. My past isn't relevant here."

Taryn took a minute to digest this, then said, "It's an existential crisis."

"Yes! Not to mention lonely and isolating."

"I can imagine," Taryn said softly. Then, "I guess I can see why you want to go back."

"Yeah. My life wasn't great and I wasn't happy. But it was mine, and I can do a lot to make things better."

"I'll talk to the professor. I'm sure he'll help you. I think he's kind of excited at the thought of someone else trying his— contraption—or whatever you want to call it."

The thought made Jen nervous. She supposed it wasn't any worse than nearly dying in a car crash, but that hadn't exactly been on purpose.

"I'll miss you, though," Taryn said sadly. "I didn't see you much after the professor had his heart attack, but after you go back I'll never be able to see you again."

"I'll miss you, too," Jen said honestly. Then she glanced at her watch. "I suppose I should get back," she said.

"Yeah, I've got some studying to do," said Taryn. "But I should be able to talk to the professor tomorrow and then I'll text you."

"Great, thank you."

When she got home, Ben was setting the table. Melanie was over at a friend's house. Her mother was in the kitchen getting dinner ready. "Oh, hi, Jen," her mother said when she walked in. "Did you have fun at Anna's?"

A wave of sadness washed over Jen. She would miss this version of her mother when she went back to her old life.

"Yeah, I had fun," she said. She went over to her mother and gave her a hug.

Her mom returned the hug. "What's that for?" she asked.

"Oh, I don't know, " Jen said. "I just felt like it." She went over and gave Ben a hug, too.

"What's wrong with you?" Ben demanded, wriggling out of her grasp.

Jen laughed. "I think you're a great little brother, that's all."

"Will you finish setting the table for me then?"

Jen laughed again. "Sure." Ben scurried off.

"That was nice of you," her mom said.

"Yeah, well, enjoy it while it lasts," Jen said lightly. She had a feeling her alter-ego didn't take over her siblings' chores.

She slept badly that night, thinking of what might go wrong. What if the professor changed his mind and refused to help her? What if his contraption wasn't safe and she died? What if she ended up, not back in her old life, but someplace horrible? This wasn't exactly tried-and-true technology the professor had here. He couldn't guarantee things would work out as expected. When she finally fell asleep, she dreamed she tried to return to her old life, only to find herself in a world where she was the sole human in a world full of house cats that all looked like Aquarius. That might not have been so bad if they were being adorable, but they were all yowling and hissing. When her alarm woke her up, she felt as if she'd hardly slept at all.

She half-slept through her classes. She supposed it didn't matter anymore.

At lunch she checked her cell phone for messages. Taryn had texted, asking if 8:00 that evening would work for her.

Eight o'clock that evening. Jen's stomach dropped. By tonight, she might be back to her old life. How long would the journey take? She supposed time would be meaningless in the wormhole, but she wondered how long it would seem to her.

She could be back to her old life, or dead.

She gulped audibly. Miguel, sitting across from her, asked, "What's wrong?"

"Uh, nothing," she said. "Why would you think something's wrong?"

"You looked nervous all of a sudden."

She smiled, convincingly, she hoped. "Nothing's wrong. Really."

Miguel didn't look convinced, but he let it go. Jen texted back to Taryn, "8 is good. Pick me up at 7:30. Thanks."

She then regarded the kids seated at the lunch table. She would never see them again in this context. She might never see Miguel again at all. She hadn't met him in her old life and he might not even exist in that universe. Tears suddenly blurred her vision.

Miguel noticed. "Are you *sure* you're okay?" he asked.

She pasted on a smile. "Yes, definitely."

He didn't look convinced at all, but at least he stopped asking.

When lunch was over, they walked to their next classes together. When she reached her class, she turned and gave Miguel a hug. She had never done that before.

"What's that for?" Miguel asked. He was clearly surprised, but he was smiling.

"For being a good friend."

***

After school, she helped Melanie start dinner for the last time. Their mother was working late. Before going upstairs, ostensibly to do homework, she gave Melanie a hug, too.

"Why are you hugging me?" Melanie asked suspiciously. "Do you want to borrow money or something?"

Geez, why was everyone so suspicious of a hug?

"No, I just felt like it. I don't mean to freak you out or anything, but you're a great little sister."

"Oh, well—thanks." Jen could tell Melanie was pleased despite herself.

Upstairs, Jen finished her half-hour or so of homework. She decided not to bother practicing her flute, since she wouldn't be here tomorrow. She wanted to do something else, though. She booted up her laptop.

She wasn't sure exactly what would happen when she went back to her old life, but since everyone here had apparently been dealing with an alternate version of herself who really was thirteen in 2012, she figured an alter ego would somehow come back once she left. She hoped so, anyway. It would be horrible for her family and friends if she simply vanished.

But she figured her alter ego would be disoriented at first, after having been gone from this universe for about three months. She wanted to try to help her by bringing her up to speed on recent events. She decided to leave a note on her computer. Entitled

"Read This", it would be saved in the Documents file. She doubted anyone in her family would be searching through her Documents file between now and tomorrow morning. Jen would also leave a brief note on the bedside table, instructing the other Jen to check her computer.

After several false starts, she managed to write a note that didn't sound too crazy. She wrote about the student council election, about Anna and Isabel and Miguel. Especially Miguel, though she struggled with what to say about him. She hadn't even been sure what to say about herself at the beginning, but finally decided to be honest—her alter ego would think things were pretty crazy anyway. She had written:

I know this is crazy, but somehow we switched universes and I am an older version of you. I looked just like you, but in my mind I was thirty-seven years old and had a totally different background, though I did have the same parents and siblings, just in an earlier time. I am writing this to let you know what has happened while you've been gone. I don't know how much time has passed for you. You might even have been in a coma this whole time, if you switched places with me, since I was hit by a car.

About Miguel, she wrote:

He seems to be a good guy. We were just friends even though he wanted more, because in my head I was so much older than him. I told him I had a boyfriend named Elijah back in Seattle. But, you might like him as more than a friend. It's up to you of course, but I think he would be a good choice.

What to say about Lucy? She could avoid saying anything, but what if Lucy came back into Jen's life in some unexpected way? If she didn't warn her, the other Jen would be blindsided. She ended up summarizing the situation, saying Lucy wasn't talking to her at the moment but adding that she just wanted her alter-ego to be aware of the situation in case Lucy came back into her life somehow.

Sorry if I created an enemy for you. But I doubt she will bother you. You have some good friends at school and I don't think Lucy will be able to change their opinion of you or anything, even if she were to come back someday. She probably won't.

Should she give her alter-ego some advice? Maybe she wouldn't appreciate it. But, it might help the younger Jen to read some words of wisdom from an older version of herself, as long as she didn't sound too preachy. She might be able to save her younger self from making similar mistakes in the future. It was worth a try, anyway.

I want to tell you about my adult life. Reading about how things turned out for one version of yourself might lead you to make different (hopefully better) decisions in the future. But, of course it is your life and you should make your own decisions.

I'm getting divorced. I got married at age thirty-five, partly because I was worried that if I didn't get married soon, I would lose out on my chance to have kids. I convinced myself I was in love and the marriage lasted less than two years.

My point is, don't give yourself deadlines. You don't want to commit to something as serious as marriage because you're afraid of being alone, or you're afraid you'll miss out on having kids. Divorce is no fun, believe me, and you don't want to bring kids into an unstable situation.

In my "real" life I'm a teacher; in fact, I teach at the school you currently attend, albeit in different universes. Bizarre, huh?

I bring this up in order to warn you. Education is a noble profession. And it can be very rewarding. You just have to be okay with being broke. And getting blamed for all of society's ills. And everything is getting harder, with No Child Left Behind and school districts scrambling to make Adequate Yearly Progress. I won't go on about how misguided all of THAT is. When you get to college, things might be totally different anyway. I will say if you MUST go into education, plan on getting your master's. It might be required by the time you get there anyway, but more education equals better pay.

And while you shouldn't choose your career based solely on money, you should also be aware that money DOES buy happiness, at least to some extent. True, it can't buy you love, friends (not true friends anyway), respect, other intangibles, but it does buy you a certain amount of freedom.

She told the other Jen a few things before she decided the letter was finished. As she shut down her computer, her mother called her for dinner. When had her mother gotten home? Jen usually heard her come in through the front door, but tonight she'd been so intent on writing her letter that she hadn't even noticed. She also hadn't realized it was already 6:00.

At dinner she asked her mom if she could go study at Anna's. She was relieved her mother didn't hassle her about it. She didn't want to have to sneak out. Her mom did ask if she needed a ride, and she said, "No, her older sister is picking me up at about 7:30." That way it wouldn't look weird if anyone in her family happened to catch a glimpse of Taryn in her car when she arrived.

"Don't stay out too late," her mother said. "It's a school night."

Jen hesitated for the briefest moment, then said, "Okay." No one seemed to notice, but her mother's words caused her a brief moment of panic. She hoped the other Jen would be there to take her place. She wished she could check somehow, but as far as she knew, she couldn't.

After dinner she helped with the dishes and then waited anxiously for Taryn to arrive. She couldn't read or surf the Internet or do anything else. She had already finished her homework just so it would be done for the other Jen. She dragged her desk chair up by the window and watched for Taryn's car.

The second she pulled up, Jen raced downstairs, grabbed her jacket and yelled, "Bye!", and ran out the door.

"You're in a hurry," Taryn observed as Jen slid into the front seat. "It's like I'm driving a getaway car."

Jen laughed nervously. "I told my parents I'm studying with a friend tonight," she said. "And I didn't want them to see that I don't have any books. Plus, I guess I'm just nervous. "

"You can still back out, of course, if you've changed your mind."

"I don't want to back out. I'm just nervous, like I said. And I'll admit it was a little sad, knowing I wouldn't see anyone—my friends, my family—again in this context."

"Yeah, of course," Taryn said. She was quiet for a moment. Then she said, "Could you do me a favor?"

"Um, I could try." What favor could Taryn be asking for at this point?

"When you get to—where you're going, home, or however you think of it, will you check and see if some version of me exists there?"

"Sure, I guess. What do you want me to say to her, though?"

Taryn thought for a moment. "Well, I'd like for you to tell her your story, but I'm not sure how you can convince her it's true. "

"I'm not sure how either," Jen admitted. "I think it would depend on what I found. If I found someone pretty much like you are now, I could tell her details about your/her life that I would otherwise have no way of knowing. I could tell her about how the professor helped me and if he exists there pretty much like he does here, that would help convince her."

"Worth a try," Taryn said.

"I'll do what I can."

They spent the rest of the drive going over details in Taryn's life—her parents, places she'd lived, her siblings. Jen didn't mind, though. It took her mind off herself and the journey she would soon be taking. They weren't sure how the details of another Taryn's life might compare to this one, so Jen might need to apply a shotgun approach to find something that resonated. She did wonder about one thing. "I will try to do this for you. But you do realize I probably won't be able to communicate with you to tell you I've found another Taryn?"

"I know," Taryn agreed. "Don't worry about it. But if you do find another me and another version of the professor, they may try to contact us. Maybe he's already tried to communicate with alternate versions of himself. He didn't tell me and I didn't think to ask. We can ask him when we see him. But I just want any other version of me who might exist to know it's possible to travel to parallel universes and through time. If she doesn't already know."

"I see. I'll do what I can."

They were now in front of Dr. Murphy's house. Jen gulped nervously as Taryn parked. Taryn reached over and squeezed her hand. "You'll be okay," Taryn said. Jen smiled weakly. They couldn't be certain of that until Jen was safely "home", but she appreciated Taryn's attempt to reassure her.

The professor greeted them at the door. To Jen, he seemed to be pretty much back to his usual self. He was maybe a little paler than the last time she'd seen him, but otherwise he looked okay. After he greeted Taryn he said, "Jen, it's good to see you again."

"It's good to see you, too, Dr. Murphy," Jen replied, hoping her voice didn't sound shaky. "I'm glad you have been recovering well."

"Thank you, Jen. They thought I was a goner for awhile, but I don't give up easily. And I'm glad to be able to help you, if you're sure that's what you want."

"I'm sure," said Jen. They were walking toward the back of the house, in the direction of the lab. "But I do have some questions."

"I'll be happy to answer any questions," the professor said. "I want to make sure you understand what you're getting yourself into."

Jen tried to ignore the pang of alarm in her head. His words weren't unexpected. He had warned her before, after all.

In the lab, they all sat down, the professor at a computer chair and Jen and Taryn on a couch in one corner of the large room. The professor's chair had wheels, and he turned it around to face them.

"Jen, this is a really big decision you've made, and you said you had some questions. I'll answer all your questions, but before I do, can you answer one for me?

Jen blinked. "I can try."

"You don't have to tell me if you'd rather not, but why did you decide to go back? I mean, I can understand missing your old life, I guess, even if you weren't happy at the time. But here you still get to have your same family and an extra twenty-five years or so of life, an extra twenty-five years of youth! Many people would give their eye teeth for such an opportunity. Not to mention the chance to do things over, and maybe be happier with your life this time around."

"I considered that, Professor, I really did. But that's just it. This really isn't *my* life. It's someone else's. And that someone may be a younger version of me, but she isn't me, not really. She didn't have my life experiences. And I can't talk about my real life experiences—anything before about three months ago—with anyone except you and Taryn, unless I want to be institutionalized. As I told Taryn, it's like I didn't exist at all until I was unceremoniously dumped into this universe."

"She s having an existential crisis, just like you said she might," Taryn chimed in.

"Fascinating," the professor said.

"You said you've traveled throughout the multiverse," Taryn said to the professor. "Have you ever met up with an alternate version of yourself?"

The professor hesitated a moment before answering. Then he said, "I have deliberately avoided doing so. I wasn't sure what would happen. I thought it might violate some law of physics that would destroy both me and my other self. Also, I did consider the possibility of some shift in consciousness—as what apparently happened to Jen. So I just didn't want to take the chance of meeting up with an alternate version of myself."

"How do you avoid it?" Taryn asked.

"Well, I can't guarantee it won't happen. I could run into "myself" almost anywhere, really. But I can use the technology I developed to communicate with other universes. I *have* actually talked with alternate versions of myself. I wasn't as worried about that, over the distance. Although—" he glanced over at Jen. "Maybe I should have been."

Jen was in awe, hearing what was possible. "But I wasn't communicating with another self when I suddenly found myself in a parallel universe."

"I know. I still can't figure out what happened in your case. The best explanation I can come up with is that your near-death experience occurring at about the same time as the other Jen's had something to do with it. But I know that explanation is woefully incomplete. You've probably heard though about how some people are never the same after near-death experiences, and maybe some of them experience something like this."

"Maybe," Jen said doubtfully. "But I've never heard anyone describe anything like this."

"Perhaps because, like you, anyone who went through anything like what you went through would be worried about being thought insane," the professor noted.

"True," Jen said.

"What other questions can I answer?" the professor asked.

"How do you know where to send me?" she asked him.

"Well, the computers in here aren't just regular computers," the professor told her. "They are extremely powerful, for one thing. And they can do things ordinary computers simply can't do. All universes have coordinates in space and time. The ones more similar to ours have coordinates that only vary slightly. Universes vastly different from ours have very different coordinates.

"I don't have the entire multiverse mapped out, of course. It's far too extensive. I know your destination universe has coordinates fairly close to ours—same year; lots of other similarities. So I'm taking what I know from my travels and communications along with what you've told me to plot the coordinates. I must warn you, however, there is necessarily a bit of guesswork involved. I think the coordinates are the best approximation possible, but you might find everything isn't exactly the same as you left it. I believe things will be close enough so you will feel comfortable. Things will make sense to you and you'll be able to share your life history with people again. Most of it, anyway."

Jen nodded. "I understand."

"Good. Now, do you have any other questions?"

"Yeah. What does it—feel like? I mean, when you're—traveling?"

The professor smiled. "It's not as scary as you might think. You will experience a falling sensation that seems like it lasts for a few seconds or so. Time is meaningless when you're actually in the wormhole. You'll probably feel a floating sensation for what will seem like a few minutes. And then you'll be there."

"When you say 'there' . . . what do you mean exactly? I mean, will I be in a lab like this one in the other universe?"

"No, you should find yourself back where that version of you in that universe is. Remember what I said before. It may violate some law of physics to have two versions of yourself in the same universe. I'm not sure. "

"Wait a minute—you don't think this will destroy me, do you?"

"I wouldn't help you go if I thought that. I've thought about it a lot since I first met you and learned your story. Of course I had been avoiding an encounter with another self as I had mentioned, because I was unsure what would happen. You managed—albeit involuntarily—to switch places with another self and not be destroyed, so it's obviously possible. And I'm also thinking, like I said, it would probably violate several laws of physics for two versions of you to exist in the same universe. But based on what happened to you before and also on my communications with others in the multiverse, I do believe it's safe to say that you will simply switch again."

Well, it wasn't any less plausible than anything else that had happened.

"So—are you ready?" the professor asked.

"I—I guess so."

"Really, I wouldn't let you go if I didn't think you'd be safe," the professor reassured her again.

"I know." She turned to Taryn. "I guess this is good-bye, then."

Taryn gave her a hug. "I'll miss you, Jen. Remember to look me up in your other world."

Jen hugged her back. "I will. I promise. And I'll miss you, too. Even if I find another 'you', it won't be quite the same."

"Yeah, exactly."

Jen turned toward the professor and the chamber. She hesitated.

"The coordinates are already programmed in," he told her. "Just step into the chamber. You'll feel like you're falling for a second or two, as I mentioned, but you'll be fine. Your journey will be nearly instantaneous."

He pressed the button beside chamber door. It slid open.

Nervously, Jen stepped into the chamber and felt herself fall.

Chapter Nineteen

Again she floated in darkness. The sensation seemed to last forever this time.

I don't remember it lasting this long last time, Jen thought. *Maybe this time I really am dead.*

But finally she had the sensation of being on something solid rather than floating. A bed. She was lying on a bed. Voices. Was that Amy talking now?

"I thought I saw her eyelids flutter." Definitely Amy's voice.

"I don't know." Jen's mother answered Amy. "It might have been wishful thinking."

"Don't be so negative!" Amy cried. "She might be able to hear you."

"Might. She MIGHT be able to hear us. We don't really know. That's what the doctor said, and I'm inclined to agree."

"Well, he also said there isn't any reason she shouldn't wake up," Amy said fiercely.

I CAN hear you! Jen thought. But she couldn't speak. She must be in a hospital. And she WAS in a coma! So—had she dreamed the whole thing after all? She couldn't navigate the confused tangle of her thoughts.

"I know," her mother whispered, her voice breaking. "I'm trying to be positive. But with every day that goes by and she doesn't wake up . . ."

"Don't even say it," Amy said, now also sounding near tears. "I can't lose my best friend."

She said best friend. So Jen was an adult, whether she'd been dreaming before or not.

"I saw it again," Amy cried. "Her eyelids definitely fluttered!"

"Jen?" her mother asked hesitantly, reaching for Jen's hand.

With all her might, Jen squeezed.

"I felt a slight pressure," her mother said. "Just slight, though . . . hey, I saw her eyelids flutter too!"

"I have to call the nurse," said Amy, pushing the call button next to Jen's bed.

Jen kept trying to squeeze her mother's hand. Her mother mentioned it once, but mostly Jen failed to exert enough pressure for her mother to notice.

After what seemed like ages to Jen, but was probably only a few minutes, the nurse arrived.

"Her eyelids fluttered!" Jen's mother and Amy said together. "And I think I felt her squeezing my hand," Jen's mother added.

"That's great," the nurse encouraged. "She seems to be showing signs of the coma lightening."

"Jen, come on, wake up," Amy coached.

Jen tried to comply. She put all of her concentration into opening her eyes. Her eyelids felt like they were made of cement. She only managed to get them about halfway open before they snapped shut again. But everyone noticed and began talking excitedly.

"Come on, Jen, you can do it," Amy coaxed.

Jen tried again. This time she managed to open them all the way. Slowly the room came into focus.

First she saw Amy. Her friend's concerned face broke into a broad grin. "Jen, you're awake! Look, her eyes are open," Amy said excitedly, turning to her right. With great effort, Jen turned her head in the same direction and saw her mother, dressed in nurse's scrubs.

"Mom?" Jen's voice was hoarse, soft, but audible. "How come you're still a nurse?"

Everyone laughed. "You're a little confused, honey, but you're awake! That's what matters." Her mother hugged Jen, and then Amy did the same.

"Wonderful!" The nurse exclaimed. "I'll inform the doctors right away." She checked Jen's vital signs and left.

"What happened?" Jen asked. Her throat felt parched. "I need water." Amy poured her a cup from the pitcher on the nightstand and handed it to her. Jen sipped slowly. Speaking was easier once she drank some.

"You were in a car accident," Jen's mother said.

"Jen, I'm so sorry I didn't wait that day to make sure your car started!" Amy said. "I'd forgotten you were having problems with it."

"It's okay," Jen said. "Don't worry about it."

"Do you remember anything about that day?" Her mother gazed at her intently.

"I think so." Jen took another sip of water. "My car wouldn't start, like Amy said, so I started to call someone, but my cell phone died and I couldn't find the car charger. Maybe Josh took it or something. Anyway, the building was already locked. Remember how we'd been talking pretty late, Amy?"

Amy nodded. "You were pretty upset."

Jen was relieved that what she remembered seemed consistent with Amy's memory, though she couldn't understand why her mother was still a nurse if she really had been dreaming.

"Anyway," Jen continued. "I left my lanyard with my ID and building key on it in my classroom, so I couldn't get in, and everyone had left. I had to find a phone, so I went to the convenience store a few blocks away. So I was walking, and even though I'd been feeling better after talking to you, Amy, I was really upset again, and I guess I wasn't paying attention, and I got hit by a car, and it seems like I knew the person who hit me—isn't that weird—can't remember who though—"

"Arabella!" Amy exclaimed. "She's been here to visit a few times. She feels horrible about it. She said she tried to stop; you weren't at a corner or anything—"

Once Amy said that, the memory slammed into Jen's consciousness, in stunning detail. "Right, Arabella hit me! I remember now. But I wasn't paying attention," Jen said again. "I'm sure it wasn't her fault."

"That's what the police determined, from eyewitnesses and everything. But still. She knew how awful you'd been feeling, thinks she should have pushed harder for you to get some help through employee assistance—"

"It's not her fault," Jen said again. "I'd given her reason to be mad at me lately."

"I've been taking care of Aquarius," said Amy. "I knew you wouldn't want Josh to do it, even though he offered."

"You're right about that," Jen agreed. "How long have I been here, anyway?"

"Eight days," her mom and Amy said together.

She must have dreamed the whole thing somehow. But how strange, to have dreamed that three months had passed, seemingly in real time. . .

Jen glanced at her mother again. "Mom, how come you're in nursing scrubs?"

Her mother looked at her strangely. "I just got off my shift at Dr. Dorian's office."

OK, several things didn't compute. She thought she had dreamed that whole strange other life in which she was thirteen years old in 2012. But in her adult world, her mother lived in Montana and worked as a secretary. She wasn't a nurse who lived in the same city in Washington as Jen did. She *had* just emerged from a coma, so she supposed some confusion was normal, but—

"Dr. Dorian?" she asked.

"I guess you might have a few memory problems at first. Hopefully nothing permanent," her mother said, glancing at her with concern. "I started this job right before your accident; that might be why you don't remember. Dr. Dorian, the pediatrician I started working for three weeks ago. You were right to suggest I move here after your dad died, Jen. My new job is great and I love being closer to you. And with Melanie in Portland and Ben in Spokane, it's perfect!"

Jen absorbed the words, trying to look as if she understood. Everything else matched. In her adult life, Melanie lived in Portland and Ben in Spokane, and their father had died not too long ago.

But her mother had been a secretary.

It could only mean one thing.

She hadn't dreamed the whole parallel-universe life she'd been living for several weeks. Nor had she come back to the exact same one she'd left.

She'd traveled to a universe similar to her old one. And that's when it hit her.

"It worked!" she said. She'd made it through the wormhole, which she now vaguely remembered. The falling sensation right before the blackness . . . Everything wasn't exactly the same, but she was an adult again and it sounded as though most things were the same.

Two pairs of eyes stared at her, puzzled.

"Jen? Are you okay? What are you talking about? What worked?" Her mother's brows knit together in concern.

"Oh, I—" Jen tried to force her still-sluggish brain to think quickly. Luckily their attention was diverted just then.

"Hey, Miguel," Amy called out, addressing someone at the door.

Jen looked over to the open doorway and saw an unfamiliar man standing there. Puzzled, she said, "Do I know you?"

"Jen, you're awake!" the man said in reply, his face lighting up. Jen gaped at him in puzzlement. As she stared at him, she realized he didn't look totally unfamiliar, with his dark, Latin good looks. And the name Miguel . . .

"Miguel?" she asked. Impossible. *Miguel was just a kid . . .*

No. That Miguel lived in a whole other universe.

Still . . . she couldn't remember ever meeting a grown-up version of Miguel. And she would remember that.

"We haven't officially met," Miguel said, coming over to stand beside her bed. "I'm Miguel Santos. Pleased to finally make your acquaintance."

"Hi," Jen said shyly. "I must look awful." Suddenly she felt very self-conscious of being in bed in a hospital gown in front of this strange man.

"Don't be silly," he said, now sounding rather shy as well. She could hear traces of the adolescent Miguel she remembered. "I hope you didn't mind my coming to visit."

"No—I don't mind. I—I feel like we've met." That much was true.

"Well, the first time we met, you had just been knocked unconscious." he said.

"Miguel just happened to be walking by when you were hit by the car," Amy explained eagerly. "If he hadn't been there to give you CPR, you probably would have died! He's your hero."

Miguel blushed at this. "Anyone would have done the same thing, Amy," he said.

"But you were the one who actually did it," said Amy. "And not everyone knows how to do CPR correctly."

"You were—there?" Jen asked, stunned.

"Yeah," said Miguel. "It was horrible. The car—Arabella is the name of the driver I guess—she tried to slow down and go around you—"

"I wasn't paying attention at all," Jen said.

"How can you even remember that?" Amy asked. "I thought people forgot things right around the time of an accident like that, especially with head trauma and all."

"I—don't know. I guess it's different for everyone." Jen supposed most people didn't travel to another universe for awhile while supposedly in a coma either, though she didn't know if that had anything to do with it. "The last thing I remember is finally looking up when Arabella honked the horn and locking eyes with her. Her face went bone white! I just froze. I even remember the motion of her arm as she jerked the wheel, trying to go around me. And the screech of the brakes. But of course she still hit me."

"That's a lot of detail," said Miguel, impressed.

"It's kind of frozen in my mind," Jen said. But then her mind went back to her original question. "So you—saved me?"

"Well," Miguel said, blushing again. "I called 911 on my cell and performed CPR until the ambulance got there."

"Well, thank you," Jen said softly. "And thank you for coming to visit me here."

"Of course. I'm really glad you're awake. We thought you might not. Wake up, that is. I thought I might not get to meet you."

What an awful eight days it must have been for her family and friends, Jen thought. She hoped she hadn't actually died in some other universe. She looked over at her mother and Amy, sitting quietly on the other side of her bed from where Miguel was standing. She got the impression they wanted her and Miguel to ignore them. Amy actually gave her a discreet thumbs up. Like she'd be thinking about dating right after she came out of a coma. But if Amy emerged from a coma and met the hot guy who had given her CPR, she would be thinking about it. That was Amy.

"Thanks for being here," she said, smiling at Amy and her mother.

"Of course," they chorused.

"Where else would we be?" her mother asked.

"We should go to the cafeteria, though," Amy said suddenly. "We haven't eaten in awhile. Right, Ruby?" she asked, touching Jen's mother's arm.

"What?" Jen's mother looked confused.

"C'mon, aren't you hungry?" Amy prodded, nudging her again.

"Oh—well, I guess, if you don't mind, Jen. We won't be long." Jen's mother still seemed confused, but she allowed Amy to lead her toward the door.

"It's fine, mom," Jen said. Amy winked at her as soon as she was out of Miguel's line of vision. It was all Jen could do not to roll her eyes.

After they left, she said, "You know, I really do feel like I've met you before."

"Really?" Miguel asked. "But how can that be? I don't think we've . . ."

"Oh, I don't know," said Jen. "You just remind me of someone I knew when I was a kid."

***

Six Months Later

Sitting on her deck, enjoying the late-morning sunshine and a hot chocolate on a Sunday, Jen contemplated her life. Before traveling to the parallel universe, she wouldn't have thought it possible for her life to change as dramatically as it had in the last six months. Nothing compared inter-universe travel, of course, but she'd made big changes.

The new universe itself had caused some of the changes. In her head she called it Universe 3.0. Many of the basics were still the same as her first one. She had the same family of origin and had Amy as a best friend, thankfully. She still taught at Riverside Middle School and owned a cat named Aquarius. Josh had still left her for Libby. A few months later, the divorce was now final. Josh lost his fight for custody of Aquarius and failed in his attempt to use her as a bargaining chip. Jen received a generous settlement, enabling her to resign from her teaching job and enroll in a creative writing program at the university. She was now working on a science fiction short story based on her experience traveling to the parallel universe, but of course no one knew how rooted in fact it was.

Universe 3.0 differed from Universe 1.0 in some important ways, though. Her mother was a nurse instead of a secretary, for example. But Jen and her siblings had grown up in Montana. Her mother had actually been a secretary until her early forties, when she went back to school to study nursing. She worked as a nurse in Montana until recently, when Jen's father, a retired teacher, had died suddenly of a heart attack, at which point she moved to Washington to be closer to her kids.

Jen wished the part about her father dying of a heart attack wasn't still true. She was happy her mother was doing so well, though. Her mother adjusted well to life in Riverside, and she loved living in the same city as Jen and fairly close to Ben and Melanie. Her mother had been especially helpful while Jen was recovering from the accident, which took several weeks.

In an attempt to keep her promise to Taryn, Jen had tried to find her and the professor, but her attempts proved unsuccessful. The professor had retired a year ago in Universe 3.0. The university wouldn't provide her with a forwarding address, but she drove out to where his house had been in Universe 2.0, the house she and Taryn had visited. There it had been out in the middle of nowhere, by itself. Here she'd failed to find it, even though she was pretty sure she had the right spot. Where his house should have been, there was nothing but sagebrush and wildflowers. An internet search had proved similarly unhelpful.

She could find no student named Taryn Westlake at the university. She'd memorized Taryn's cell number before she left and tried calling it, but in Universe 3.0 it belonged to an old man who didn't know anyone named Taryn. She'd even called all the Westlakes in the phone book, hoping maybe she or her parents had a landline, but that hadn't worked either. As for the internet, she couldn't find anyone at all named Taryn Westlake, let alone the right Taryn, though she found some Taryns who lived in a town called Westlake or went to a school called Westlake. Stymied, she'd been forced to give up her search until she could think of a new avenue to try.

Jen no longer mourned the loss of her marriage. The mourning, she realized, had never been so much about losing Josh himself so much as her grief over what she saw as a dream dying—the perfect husband, the perfect kids. She really had wished she could start over again, though she guessed she hadn't been specific enough in that wish. She'd never wished to be thirteen again. Who knew the multiverse would be such a smartass? Jen laughed to herself at the thought.

At least now she knew she could start over at any age.

As though to punctuate the point, there was a knock at her door. Oh geez, Miguel had arrived and she wasn't ready yet.

Miguel was the best part of her new life. In the hospital she learned that he visited her every day while she was in the coma. How surreal to think she had been friends with the thirteen-year-old Miguel while the adult Miguel was visiting her in the hospital in another universe. They'd come into contact at about the same time in both universes.

He continued to visit her every day until she recuperated enough to leave the hospital. A week after she got out of the hospital, they had their first real date. They'd been together ever since.

Jen let Miguel in and greeted him with a kiss. "Sorry I'm not quite ready yet," she apologized. "I'll just be a minute."

"No problem," Miguel said. "Aquarius and I can hang out."

He settled himself on the couch, and Aquarius, who adored him, immediately jumped up beside him. Jen grinned at the two of them on the couch together and went into the bedroom to finish getting ready. Aquarius had never warmed up to Josh. She certainly wouldn't have been happy if she'd had to leave Jen and live with him.

As she was about to rejoin Miguel, her cell phone buzzed. She retrieved it from the nightstand. It was a text from Lucy.

"New school doesn't suck," the text read. Jen chuckled. Coming from Lucy, this was high praise indeed.

"Happy 4 U," Jen texted back.

Lucy was another success story. Armed with information from the parallel universe, Jen had worried about Lucy's home life. Through the counselor, Carina, and Amy, who was Lucy's Language Arts teacher, Jen did some checking. She learned Lucy's mother did indeed have a boyfriend named Manual. Neither the counselor nor Amy had ever met him, but they had concerns. Lucy's behavior had deteriorated and her mother had become unreliable, difficult to reach on the phone and neglecting to show up for parent meetings. Jen managed to convey her concerns to them without arousing suspicion. She also talked to Lucy a couple of times and obtained more information. Approaching Lucy wasn't easy, but she managed. Apparently her time as an adolescent with Lucy paid off.

Then Lucy's mother showed up to parent-teacher conferences with a black eye. She'd tried to cover it up with make-up, but the heating system in the school was working overtime that day—an unusual occurrence—and she'd sweated most of it off. Amy questioned her about it and Cristina broke down, saying she and Manny were having serious problems. At this point Amy called Carina over, as the conferences were held arena-style in the cafeteria and the counselors were circulating around the room. Cristina denied knowledge of any abuse of Lucy by Miguel's hand, but Carina and Amy didn't like some of her answers to their questions, plus they knew if Manny was beating Cristina he might very well be abusing Lucy as well. They filed a report with Child Protective Services.

Fortunately they intervened before Lucy made any attempt on her life in this universe, but unfortunately Manny was an asshole here, too. Lucy was placed in a temporary foster home for a few weeks, but then the sequence of events followed a trajectory similar to what Jen had seen—Cristina went to rehab, and Lucy went to live with an aunt and attend a private school on the west side of the state. A new school which, according to Lucy's text just now, "didn't suck."

"Are you almost ready?" Miguel called to her.

"Coming," she called back.

She went to join Miguel in her new life.

www.ingramcontent.com/pod-product-compliance
Lightning Source LLC
Chambersburg PA
CBHW031324170626
46807CB00002B/559